The Shaman

and Other
Almost-Tall Tales

by Jerry Zeller

To Julia —
One of my favorite
shamans —
Peace,
Jerry

Recovery Communications, Inc.
P.O. Box 19910 • Baltimore, MD 21211 • (410) 243-8558

The stories contained in this book are works of fiction. The author does not intend for any of the characters, settings, or circumstances to represent actual persons, places, or events. Any resemblance to actual entities or living persons is purely accidental.

Permission to reprint "The Shaman" is kindly granted by *The Chattahoochee Review.*

Dedication

To Amber Tanner Zeller Isham
(1903-1997), our "Mom," who
read to us from The Bookhouse
Books until there were no more
stories to tell, then loved us
through the years we sought to
become stories of our own.

Table of Contents

Acknowledgments

Many thanks to wife Pat for reading first creations and saying those encouraging words at the right time; to my editor and friend Betsy White at Recovery Communications, Inc., for careful and creative coaching which spurred improvements; and to loyal mentor Jo Ann Adkins who has always shared her infectious confidence and courageous attitude as poems or stories struggle for final form.

And thanks to Alan Jackson, nonfiction editor of *The Chattahoochee Review,* for inviting me to "enter into" my story as he helped me to spawn "The Shaman" for publication in the *Review;* to Ray Dungan, benefactor of Recovery Communications, Inc., for helping to underwrite the book; to storyteller and priest Barbara Taylor for modeling excellence in writing and living — and for pointing out my "absence" from early versions of several tales; and to Jimmy Wall for his confidence and for reminding me of other tales from our younger days in journalism school.

Foreword

It was an especially poignant experience for me when *The Chattahoochee Review* published Jerry Zeller's "The Shaman," the first story in this collection. For a good long while I have been entrusted with segments of Jerry Zeller's writing, sometimes to blue-pencil, other times simply to enjoy. There are stories told and stories published, but the earliest I can recall was a poem, "Strawberries for My Friends." That piece became so popular with his students at Mercer University that to this day many of us admit that we smile secretly when confronting strawberries, and think, joyfully, I am one of those friends!

As students at Mercer, we knew very little of Dr. Zeller's background: only that he had been "at Emory" before Mercer, and we were aware that he wore hearing aids, thanks to the percussion of artillery in the South Pacific during World War II. I don't recall whether we had any perception of him in his role as Episcopal priest. We knew him as teacher and poet. We learned early on that while Dr. Zeller could be playful and full of whimsy in his approach to teaching, there was at the heart of it something more serious than we had ever encountered before. We found complex truth and crucial reality in abundance, all of it more memorable because of teaching methods calculated to involve us in the learning process.

As he wrote more poems and our need for a poet became important, we asked him to do a reading for us — students, professors, and other friends — at one of the many gatherings we enjoyed. I learned later that in spite of all of the congregations he had addressed as a priest, and all of the students he had addressed in the classroom, the most intimidating public appearance he ever made was in reading his own poetry that evening. But of course he turned that experience, as he has every other experience, into something of value for others and for himself. Over time, the poetry merged with his other writing so that all of his work became truer and even more vivid for his reader. It became his custom, while teaching his classes, caring for his family, and serving his church, to devote whatever portion of his life he could to writing and to writers. He served for a time as president of Georgia Poetry Society, and during his presidency the membership and the prestige of the organization grew, and the encouragement he gave other writers was inestimable.

In the opening piece in this collection we meet Bill, a shaman, a Zeller family friend and employee. As we learn more about Bill we begin to understand that we are dealing with more than one shaman, another who steps from behind the haunting description of this former "Head Ringmaster in the Center Ring" to reveal himself and all of his powers:

> Bill and I are both shamans, both aware that there is another world full of mysterious adventures and populated with spirits — a world which hangs, invisible, over the world of what we call everyday, real. By telling stories of all kinds, we bring that world into this one. We control evil spirits and fill the empty places in this life with enchanting vitality and the litanies of positive energy.
>
> We are the worshipers of myth and the creators of real adventures from the realms of fantasy. We are medicine men, storytellers, teachers, priests and sages who bring this world and the otherworld together in the moment. We are not afraid to journey into imagination, to tamper with visions. We are willing to become lost in our dreams of what might have been, what might be, and what may become. We are the shamans.

A revelatory story about our shaman goes this way: A friend of his telephoned one evening to tell him, excitedly, that her night-blooming cereus was budded, and she would like to bring it to him so that he could see the miracle of the one-night-only blossom. As she was sure he already knew, the mysterious cereus produces a bud, which on a special night, over a period of several hours, unfolds. By the time the morning sun rises, alas, the blossom will have wilted away. Jerry told her that he would like to have the flower, but he was expecting a visit from a colleague who was deeply distressed, and he might be up most of the night in a counseling session. The woman said this would be all right; she would bring the bud and go on her way.

The enormous bud, still attached to a stout smooth green stem, arrived in a cobalt-blue vase, and Jerry and his friend sat talking with the vase on the table between them. As the evening wore on, the friend's troubles spilled verbally across the table, and both men concentrated more and more on this strange blossoming. The bud, fully illuminated under the lamplight, slowly opened and became a rare and magnificent white flower almost the size of a dinner plate. They could peer into the center of it and see intricate flower-parts, again all brilliant white-on-white. After about an hour an almost overpowering fragrance filled the air around them. Later, in marveling at the blossom, Jerry said that the experience gave him the inspiration for a unique sermon illustrating how things beautiful come together to create a more important beauty. That is, after all, as it must be with the work of a shaman, else his work will have no power, no meaning.

— Jo Ann Yeager Adkins
Managing Editor, *The Chattahoochee Review*
DeKalb College

Introduction

The stories in this book are stopping places for reality. They are tiny monuments to limitation. Because every time I read them I want to rewrite them, I believe they contain the seeds of revelations unbloomed. But, unlike uncaptured existence still unclaimed, they have been captured and cannot go on beyond themselves. If they "go on," they become "something else," no matter how vaguely recognizable.

It is the reader who has the power to make them go on into something else, once I have done with them. For those who read them, they become more, though I do not change them one whit. The stories as captives to my words do not change, but the reader brings to each of them that which I could not write. Some philosophers teach that reality occurs only at the moment of perception. And each moment provides a fresh reality. A story read is a story perceived — and the reader is the master of the story at the moment it is read. It comes into being when read, and the reader recreates it all over again in a new image of reality.

In a discussion following a speech I made to a college honorary group about the myths, metaphors, and realities of "family life," one of the students exclaimed, "Why, the family disappears when the stories about it are not told any more!" My response to her was, "Yes! I think that is the way it is. Now, go and begin writing down your family story so that all of it cannot escape!" I shared with her my belief that not only would the stories carry the family's myths forward, but that it is only the myths which survive the past anyway. I think the stories in our minds recreate and continue the myths of our realities in all sectors of perceived existence. Reality is, indeed, a flimsy substance.

We say that when we are writing it, a story "unfolds." That is not so. It is imagined and then "folded," neatly and completely. That is what the author finally does with it. And that is that. It is the reader who "unfolds" with the story, gives it life and the character of a fresh, unique blossom. So the story becomes the benchmark, a direction-pointer, a locator in the vast swamp of "reality," stimulating "unfolding" for those who might read it.

And what does the storyteller write? It is always fiction, for nonfiction does not exist in recollected form. All origins end with the gasp of their occurrence. Hence, to write of the past or from one's imagination at all is to tell stories, arrange artifices, create fables or spawn tales. That is why we can say there are "almost-tall tales," for it is like an admission, an attempt at honesty, to declare that nothing written is in pristine form or can report the exact subject or object of its contents. Yet, we must also respect that in the tale there is the energy of some reality that has continued, miraculously showing itself in a new appearance. Like the larger realities of myths themselves, tales are not reality but carry on or perpetuate the echo-image of an earlier reality. Surely, this must be so of the enduring tales and myths found, for example, in all religious traditions.

What fun! What joy! We must tell stories and delight in them, lest we disappear and have no consolations for our journeys. We must, with devotion and expectation, construct our "almost-tall tales," revisiting them from time to time for new messages about the mystery of life itself.

— Jerry Zeller
February 1998

The Shaman

I've tried to probe the place in my consciousness that makes Bill's death hang about me, as if his shroud fitted some part of me that I'm not certain of. He knew in fact something that I know but don't remember that I know, a realm of life that is real but touching the border of mystery, otherworldliness.

When I was a boy I spent time hanging around the family restaurant, "helping." That's where everyone mostly stayed. I can't remember the rooms in our various apartments or houses. They mix together as unimportant, like the names and faces of most of my teachers at school. But the restaurant I remember, inch by inch, bucket by bucket, table by table, chair by chair, door by door. And Bill.

Bill and his wife, Sarah, worked there. They managed the spaces that my mother and father could not cover. They became "family." Of course, there was paternalism from my father and maternalism from my mother, but that was expected in those days. That's how a family business became a family. There were responsibilities enough for everyone. The owners knew theirs, managers knew theirs, counter girls knew theirs, kitchen helpers knew theirs, and the cleaning man knew his.

Bill was a member of the family. But there was more. Like some clever uncle who was beloved but "a little strange," he poured potions of enchantment into everything he did. One cigarette after another always surrounded his face with a haze of ghostly wisps, transfiguring the present into memories taking comfortable shape away from their accustomed time.

When he spoke, it was like gravel grating out words wrapped in newly created sounds. When he whispered, it was like the intimate scratch of fine sandpaper planing the smooth surface of secrets a boy should touch and hear.

Bill's sandwiches were the model for others who tried. When he waited on customers, they thought they had just been anointed with the chrism of personal love. When he swiped a counter clean with a steaming towel, the surface became translucent for an instant. And when Bill checked the cash register or summed up the day's paperwork, it was as if he were conducting the discordant instruments of the netherworld with the powerful baton of his personal optimism. When he had tamed them into symphonic accord, his eyes would gleam through the mists of smoke, victorious.

Bill knew the mind of a boy. He knew me better than Mom and Dad in many ways. He knew early in our friendship that I was a reader of stories, that I already had the gift of leaving this world for the spell-binding world past, of reaching into the ever-changing dreams of exotic otherness. Intuitively, I knew that Bill had already been in all those places, and he knew that I knew. And so when the lunch crowd was gone and I was in the way more than ever, he would take me out on the back steps by the garbage cans, light up a fresh cigarette, and tell me tales.

I learned years later that Bill grew up in poverty in a milltown village. But that was not the "real" boyhood that he shared with me. "Actually," he had traveled with the circuses and Wild West shows as a little boy and young man. His father herded buffalo for Buffalo Bill Cody's Wild West Show. Bill went all over America and the continent of Europe. He even shook hands with the King of England, at least once. His mother cooked fresh deer meat every day for Buffalo Bill's lunch and trimmed his beard with his scalping knife — the sharpest knife in the world. One slip and she would have ended it all for Buffalo Bill, and she always had to tell him to sit still.

And then they went to work for the Ringling Brothers and Barnum and Bailey Circus. His father made it possible for Clyde Beatty to do his dangerous act with lions and tigers, for he could hypnotize a wild lion in two seconds and saved Clyde Beatty's life nearly every day. Bill's mother was chief chef in the circus kitchen and became famous feeding all the midgets, clowns, tightrope walkers, trapeze artists, trick riders, and the tent gangs. That's where Bill got his knack for restaurant work, from his mother.

One day Bill's mother was messing around with some new ideas in the kitchen when she accidentally discovered one of the most important things in circus history: how to make cotton candy! She sold the recipe to Mr. P. T. Barnum at his request, retired from hard kitchen work forever, and spent her last years riding like a queen on the top of elephants, wearing a great African headdress she made out of real ostrich feathers.

During those days Bill was growing up, learning to be the Master of Ceremonies and Head Ringmaster in the Center Ring. He wore a top hat and tuxedo all the time and was in charge of announcing all the acts on schedule and keeping everyone in their proper places. He had a cane that had an ivory head carved with the face of a witch doctor — with strands of the witch doctor's real hair coming out of the top! Bill was definitely the most important person in the entire circus.

Until he had his accident. It wasn't his fault. They didn't put enough powder in the cannon and shot the Human Cannonball straight at him. When he came to in the hospital, he learned that the Human Cannonball had not survived, but the chinstrap from his helmet had lodged in Bill's throat, causing him to forever after speak in a raspy voice. Of course, after losing his beautiful and much-admired voice, he could no longer be Master of Ceremonies. So he left the circus and . . . but that's another bunch of stories.

From time to time, Bill would, as he said, "go on furlough" from the restaurant. I could tell Sarah didn't like it much when he was to go. She wouldn't say anything to him, his teasing her would get out of hand, and my father would finally tell Bill he would see him when he got back. I never knew in those days where he went. He'd be gone for weeks at a time, and when he returned he'd be sunburned almost red and so full of energy that my father had to slow him down to a trot.

Those were the days when I wished I could go somewhere else, too. Maybe even go with Bill — but I was afraid to suggest it. Instead, I would hike to the top of Billygoat Hill and look across the Missouri River into Kansas. I wondered if Bill might be roaming around over there, watching the sun set behind a thundering herd of buffalo, or maybe working in a circus in the Center Ring. I wanted to be with him, wherever he was. I knew he would teach me magic things and show me worlds of fantasy far superior to school and being just a plain boy. I could help him fight evil, survive all hardships, and always win for the good guys like us.

I went back home for Bill's funeral. I looked at him in his white casket. Lung cancer had thinned and faded his leathery face. Yet I wanted to reach over and raise his eyelids. I waited for his lips to move and grate out a brand-new story. I knew that he was on another of his adventures, a "furlough," and I felt the same old impulse to run away with him, to follow him wherever he was going. I knew his eyes were dancing under those lids, that he was already somewhere wonderful, spinning yarns and creating a world to match them. He would never meet a stranger in any world.

My thoughts began to spread through the pathways of my own life. Through the years, I, too, had become a dabbler in the occult, a trafficker in the business of unknown worlds. Between Bill's storytelling and his death, I had traveled far beyond Kansas, high above the dusty buffalo herds and westward toward the never-setting sun. Sometimes in my mind. Sometimes in fact.

I had traveled through a vast world war that was more danger-ous and bizarre than a Wild West show. Battle stars appeared upon my chest. A Philippine Liberation Ribbon became a window through which I can still, in unwonted moments, watch the human herds stampeded by the excitement of hatred and violence. I was just a boy. But I was not too young to notice that the dirty, festering corpse of a Japanese soldier lay on the soil of paradox, his final bed surrounded by some of the most beautiful mountains and forests I would ever see. When enemy night fires twinkled high on the dark, mysterious volcanic cones, I learned to expect the theatrical explosions of a tropical dawn and to hope for the creation of a better world.

As an artilleryman, I learned the deadly ways of cannon wands. We called them howitzers. Bill's cannon story swept through my panic when I suddenly lost the high frequencies of my hearing. I remembered that, according to his tale about losing his voice, Bill's life was changed. But he not only survived — he became my friend and the greatest storyteller I knew. I began to learn to read lips. I vowed to survive, too.

In time, I became an Episcopal priest, a ringmaster under the towering tent of the Church. The mysteries of another world touched my fingers through sacraments of water, wine, and bread. Vestments flowed from my shoulders like otherworldly costumes, symbols of being more than I could be. Venerable stories sprang from my lips. I joined the boisterous processions of faith, up one aisle and down another, seeking connections between now and then.

Later, I craved more freedom, a wider scope for probing questions and answers. I learned the craft of a college professor. With my initiation into the world of academe came new robes, new titles — and more mysteries. As teacher and continuous learner, I believed in the transforming magic of research and knowledge, herding the unruly minds and spirits of students ever "onward," ever toward the dawns and sunsets of fact and fantasy. Always fascinated, unsettled by new discoveries, my meaning depended upon the excitement of floating through the fluid spaces between what I knew and what I might know.

Realization came slowly as the years refused to jell into a final, inert conclusion. I knew joy, for I had survived the accidents that had changed my senses, given me life with a different ear, excluded me from one thing and propelled me into another. I benefitted by taking "furloughs," by visiting beyond the borders of the mundane, by searching for the places where what is real embraces what might become. And I had grasped the enthusiasm of returning to my daily chores, energized and refreshed by the spirits who dwell in other places.

Then I knew. I knew what it was that we had both known together. Bill and I are both shamans, both aware that there is another world abounding in mysterious adventures and populated with spirits — a world that hangs, invisible, over the world of what we call everyday, real. By telling stories of all kinds, we bring that world into this one. We control evil spirits and fill the empty places in this life with enchanting vitality and the litanies of positive energy.

We are the worshipers of myth and the creators of real adventures from the realms of fantasy. We are medicine men, storytellers, teachers, priests and sages who bring this world and the otherworld together in the moment. We are not afraid to journey into imagination, to tamper with visions. We are willing to become lost in our dreams of what might have been, what might be, and what may become. We are the shamans.

I confess that I have never ceased to travel through Kansas, over the rumbling buffalo herds and into the setting sun with Bill's spirit at my side, his affectionate, raspy voice in my ear. Even though I came to know the difference between the fiction of Bill's tales and the reality of his childhood in a bleak, abusive milltown, I have known from the time of his conjuring tutorials that life is a circus and it is my home, the Greatest Show on Earth.

And I must tell my children and their children how it was, being brought up with Bill's tales to clothe my innocence in the enduring weave of mystery and reality. They must know what it is like to sit amid garbage cans on the back steps of the family restaurant and travel to the ends of the earth. To be caught in the confused excitement of a Wild West show. To shake the hand of a king. To be part of an unbelievably amazing circus.

After the funeral, I asked Sarah where Bill used to go on his many "furloughs." She laughed and said that when he couldn't stand the confining restaurant scene a minute more, he would leave to join a traveling carnival. He owned his own cotton-candy machine and would follow the carnival through villages and small towns, selling his cones of pink, sticky sweetness, telling stories of his old days with Buffalo Bill and with the Greatest Show on Earth, cementing this world with the other. Then, refreshed and confirmed, he'd come home to Sarah, the restaurant, and, fortunately, to me.

On "furlough" again, I am certain Bill is doing the thing we shamans always try to do: bring two lost worlds together. It's a task as sweet as cotton candy, as magnificent as a stampeding herd of buffalo, and as exciting as a circus with three rings. ✹

The Lucky Mitt

The day finally came when Dad let me try on his third baseman's glove. He called it his "Lucky Mitt" and said it would be mine and bring its luck along, if I would keep growing up. When he handed it to me, I heard a buzzing in my ears, and my hands seemed suddenly to become fumbly and inept. My youth's hand hesitated like my heartbeat. Was I ready to climb to a higher league? Could I make it? Could I live up to the expectations required by such an awesome symbol?

Could I really wear it when we played catch in the street? What would the other boys say when they saw me soar like the tail of a comet, chase a sailing sphere through the universe, nab it on the outer fringe of left field, and yes, actually make the last great catch of the World Series?

It was no normal mitt. From the beginning of time and of baseball, Dad's long, strong fingers had kneaded saddle soap into its leather until it was supple and shiny, almost alive to the touch. He had worn it through the ragged clashes on the rough pasture diamonds of the minors. I had watched from the shadows of my childhood imagination, cheering him on as he spread the "good old days" before my childhood dreams. There had always been the magical Lucky Mitt, and now I was to be allowed to wear it!

In its palm was a very important hole. Dad had cut out a perfectly round piece from the mitt, half the size of a baseball. He told me how his skin had blistered and then toughened in his palm as he shagged fierce bullets roaring down the third-base line. He explained how the hole helped to trap the ball until he could master it and send it sizzling on its way to first base.

Four flat fingers spread like pudgy rays from the sunken, sun-shaped hole. A blocky thumb hung off at an awkward angle, waiting to be filled and animated by my Dad, an outside genius beyond its control.

It was his Lucky Mitt. And it was my Lucky Day. I gingerly poked my small hand into the slot under the strap. But my un-finished fingers could not make it to the end of the dark passages designed for them, and the thumb was simply beyond my reach. I lacked the mature strength of hand that could fold the glove into a cup for catching. It seemed to hang on the end of my slender arm, a lifeless mass, begging for the inspiration of action I could not provide. I felt inadequate, even dead.

But Dad said it looked great on me. He wasn't at all con-cerned that it didn't yet fit. I would grow into it — that he promised me. He said I could practice wearing it all afternoon, and then came the big surprise! I could go into the living room with The Men after Sunday dinner. I could join my grandfather and my uncles and my older cousins, hunched around the radio, listening to the St. Louis Cardinals' play-by-play. I could wear the Lucky Mitt the whole time. I could be a man!

It was like being born into another world, for the spectators in our living room, whenever they disagreed with the manager's strategy, would shout at one another in German. There were at least three and sometimes as many as seven better opinions. They joined forces only to curse the umpires — "blind as bats," they declared, and obviously "out to kill the Cards."

I listened as if hearing the sound of Creation for the first time, and I learned about fury and loyalty and hysteria and joy and shame and amusement and hope. Without noticing what was happening, I became a lover of major-league baseball. Through the dimly lighted dial of our old humpbacked radio, I could "see"

them all — players, umps, and fans — performing together somewhere deep within the polished brown box. With inner revulsion,
I could almost touch the blind, skulking, ominous umpires who
were determined to discredit my beloved "Redbirds." I was hooked
for life. No longer a boy, I became A Fan.

Somehow, the fabulous glove was "lost" in the confusion of
the Great Depression. I always suspected Dad sold it or traded it
for money to pay the rent. He never said. But he told me not to
worry about it, and taught me to catch barehanded, so I wouldn't
lose my touch. He said when he was a boy there hadn't been any
gloves for kids. "You can play the game without a glove," he
said, "and then you appreciate it more when you've got one."

Dad never lived to attend a World Series game in person. In
his later years, after he transplanted our roots from Missouri to
Atlanta, I used to take him out to see the Braves. "They never
should have moved from Boston!" he lamented, when they were
horrible and he was eighty. He muttered under his breath in
German at needless errors. He winced when they took the pitcher
out — "Let him stay in there 'til he works it out! What kind of
babies are these guys?" He cursed out loud in English so the
umpires would understand that he considered them the biggest
bums in Christendom.

And then came the year when the Braves won it all. Dad
has long been gone for good. But he would have approved of
the rosy-cheeked rookie's play at third base, and his persistence
at the plate. He would have commended the graceful adagio of
the tall black veteran at first, along with his lethal bat. And he
would have smiled and nodded his head when the pitchers pitched
like they meant it, hanging in there against the best offensive
lineups in the sport.

He would have proclaimed each game "world class," because
baseball is at its best in the climax of a pitchers' duel. Strategy
becomes all-important. Minute by minute, any decision can win

it or lose it. "You've got to be able to think," he would say, "if you want to understand baseball. Only the dummies come to see a slugging contest."

Dad used to like to sit somewhere along the third base line. That way it was easier for him to offer advice to the player at "his" position. He's too deep for the bunt. He's too close for the right-hander. He's too tight on the bag. The rookie didn't know he missed my Dad's help.

I didn't see the World Series from the field — only on TV. But my son was there. A sports producer, he was on the field with his news crew on that wonderful day of victory. He and his crew were among the first nonplayers to make it to the celebratory pile-up on the mound.

It was wild, he tells me. World Champions! Our own World Champs! I am glad that my son was raised with the Braves. Almost as glad as being raised with the Cards. He was beside me when his idol Hank Aaron broke the Babe's home-run record, and now he has lived to see his team win the Series. I am trying, now, to remember how the Cards did this year. I guess the Braves have become my team, too.

Dad would have been pleased. "Not as good a team as some of the Cardinal teams in the Thirties," he would have said, "but still, pretty damn good." And he would have said he wished he could find his Lucky Mitt, the one with the soft touch and the hole in the palm. Let him out there and he'd show the youngsters a thing or two.

I, too, wish we could find the old mitt. I grew enough to get my hand into it before it was "lost." It really was a magic glove. It could snag a hot one without thinking. It became a live part of my arm, leading me unerringly to the ball.

But above all, that mitt was my ticket into the Big Leagues, into masculinity in my family, into the hurly-burly of the adult world, into the week-in week-out struggle for the pennant, into the roar of the crowded stadium. It led me to love the shouting, the mayhem, the hot dogs, the cursing, the cheering, the frustrations, the winning, the losing — all the thrills of playing the game of life at my own position. Barehanded, if necessary.

Soon it will be time for Dad's great-grandchildren to join the adults in the living room after dinner. We'll have the game on TV, but what will we do for a Lucky Mitt? Maybe it will turn up, just in time, so that every child can try it on. Yes, that mitt, the one with the hole in it, just too big for young hands, but full of the power that kids can grow into. ✴

The Morning Rabbit

T he brown-and-gray rabbit sprang from the scraggle-land at the edge of our lawn, cast dark eyes about to make sure his suspicion of safety was correct, and inched over into a patch of grass that needed mowing. He munched. I watched. The morning framed him — moistly, softly, and graciously.

Thor and Freyja, my two large retriever dogs, were around at the other side of the house, wagging at the back door, declaring it was nibble-time in the early-morning ritual that belonged to us alone. Bent on their own compulsive schedule, they missed the chase of the day. I know about that. I wondered if the rabbit knew, as I knew, that habit clouds our sight, dulls our smell, stuffs-up our ears.

But if you know another's habits, you can create your own paths of safety. You don't have to make a big thing of it. You don't have to go to counseling or probe deep dungeons of motives. However, if you wish, you can use your knowledge to get into or out of messes with others. Because you know a lot about them, you can be there, waiting. You can get in their way or lead them on a merry chase. It might be fun. It might be dangerous.

I took binoculars from a drawer in the den. The rabbit jumped closer to my eyes. I was trying to discover his habits. I watched him eat for a little while. Then he looked about through those dark round eyes. Struck by a sudden thought (surely rabbits think!), he scampered quickly into a scattering of nearby magnolia leaves, pushed and shoved them around for a moment, didn't find what he was looking for, and plodded in lazy hops back to the patch of grass. He munched some more.

A prissy mockingbird landed close by. He didn't seem to like that, thought it over, then popped away into the underbrush of the lot next door. Predictable. Then he popped right out again. Not predictable. The mockingbird had business elsewhere and flew away. Predictable. The rabbit popped back into the underbrush. Not predictable.

By the time the morning rabbit had disappeared for what I calculated to be the last time, I reviewed the information I had collected about rabbit habit. I am a skilled social scientist, so I knew exactly how to proceed. But there really wasn't anything in my notes that I could plot, chart, or report with certainty. To make matters worse, that rabbit popped back in and popped back out again while I made more notes!

I searched my data for habits — maybe the morning rabbit always came out in the morning. But I hadn't seen him every day, and I often looked. Besides, he looked a great deal like the afternoon rabbit, and the afternoon rabbit looked a great deal like the evening rabbit. And they were not predictable either.

Having come to no conclusions, I set aside my rabbit studies for a bit and went to open the kitchen door. The dogs came roaring in, banging around the kitchen with their excited tails. Freyja walloped the trash can against the refrigerator. Thor knocked over the brass storm lantern that had been sitting on the floor to send it crashing against the wall. Predictable. I yelled at them both: "NO!" Predictable. They settled down on their haunches, draped their tongues out of their mouths, and drooled. Predictable.

I gave them their nibbles. Predictable. They went to the door, turned around, and looked straight at me. I opened the door. They charged out to see if the rabbit was around. Predictable. It wasn't. Predictable.

Thor and Freyja were trained — to a certain extent. They were trained to expect routine behavior from me. I realized, with alarm, that they had trained me too. Let me out. Let me in. Feed me at six.

Brush me in the morning. Walk me in the afternoon. I was as trapped in their — our? — habits as they were.

I became more confused. Whose habit was whose? I wondered about the morning rabbit. He was unpredictable. Or at least I did not know what to expect from him. Except that I knew I could not know exactly what he was going to do next. Predictable unpredictableness.

Suddenly I realized that the rabbit had me trained, while I did not have him trained. I was in the habit of watching for him. I was in the habit of getting the binoculars out of the drawer. I was hooked on his unpredictability. As he hopped about helter-skelter from the lot next door into my yard — and back and forth and round about — he seemed utterly free to do as he pleased.

I thought, briefly, about catching him in a clever, humane rabbit trap. Then I could train him, and he would be predictable. I would be free from his control, because I would have him well trained. When I said, "Hop," he would hop. When I said "Munch," he would munch. When I said, "Chase the mockingbird," he would chase it.

Then I remembered how the dogs had made habit-meat out of me. Forbid! I would soon be employed by the rabbit to supervise his regular hopping schedule. I would have to come home from work to provide his munchies for his munching time. And I would have to train a mockingbird to fly into my yard so that he could chase it.

It's taken steel-tough determination on my part, but I have decided once and for all to stop wondering what the morning rabbit is going to do next. When I see him, I will enjoy him. Whatever he does will be all right with me. I will respect his freedom if he will respect mine. I will not try to trap him and teach him better habits — like munching with his mouth closed, or hopping in a straight line. That is, if he won't invade my world with his own demands.

I decided that we would make a deal. I'll promise not to try to predict what that morning rabbit will do tomorrow, or in the next minute. The morning rabbit will promise to allow me complete freedom to watch, without wondering. And the same promise goes for the afternoon rabbit, and yes, for the evening rabbit too. You can count on it. It's utterly predictable. I think. ✸

Two Windows on the Street

I stood defiantly in the middle of the railroad tracks. The boy in me came rushing back, pretending danger and heroism. I would face the mighty engine without fear, I said.

I had stopped on the tracks on the way home from the post office. The letters I had salvaged from the junk mail in my box were tucked into my belt so I could swing my arms freely and have a brisk walk. It was dark in the village, late and heavily warm. A muttering thunder cursed on the other side of the Beacon Mountain ridge, still a long way off. Far enough away to allow me to walk up the hill past the old Victorian house, turn the awkward bend at the crest, then coast down the other side to my cottage. Before the rain.

I do this, sometimes — a late night walk to the post office, just to get out of the house and frisk my thoughts in the haunted night air of the village. I seldom see a soul. The village is empty of the present. Sometimes, like tonight, I play suicide with the trains that never come down the tracks any more. I pretend I am in that older age. The Past. Before rust could form on the rails. The age of glistening rails, polished by the crushing whirs of ponderous, spinning wheels.

"Come get me, monsters!" I shout up-track and down. "Oh, Past Days," I tease, "come rushing toward me. Shake the ground as giants do. Frighten me enough to want to live. Make me run for my life! Run for tonight! Run for this moment I now have!

Roar over me, steaming, screeching, dreadnoughts of Memory. If you can!"

Was it from that Memory I first heard the sound? I had heard a woman screaming as I left the post office. Almost echo-sounding, muffled, it seemed to come from deep inside the decrepit old hotel across the street. It was such a long, crying scream — not of pain but of hopelessness or despair. I waited for some activity, a light in a window or some calls or shouts. When nothing followed, I started my walk home. The scream followed me at a distance.

Having won my game with the freight train, I turned up the hill. The sound of the woman's wail came again into my consciousness, now like the distant, moaning whistle of a night train. It fixed itself into my thoughts and would not leave. As I approached the great shadow of the Victorian house the wind began to pick up. The storm had hurdled the ridges and was coming swiftly toward the village. I began to jog as I passed the house. At that instant I thought I saw a faint light filling the turret window, high among the branches of the ancient oaks that crowded the yard.

Perhaps the light was only a reflection of the lightning beginning to fall about the street. I could not tell. Rain splatters began to strike me with warning force. Breathless, I reached my cottage porch, slouched into a chair, closed my eyes, and listened to the sounds of the storm. Struggling through it all, the violence and rage of the storm, the voice of the woman's despair filled my soul with a story I have always known:

The spare, gray woman sat immobile and hushed before the ample window of the turreted sewing room. Long ago sewing had become the task of others, no longer art of the home. Somewhere, tucked into cottages in the village below, the remnant sewing ladies lived, still to be summoned up the hill to the big houses when needed, but offered only the lower rooms near the kitchen as space for work. Now, this poised, windowed room, with its welcome to light, had become a study, a retreat, filled with books, statues, vases and copies of culture, an exclusive, inert symbol of the educated and the privileged.

She sat, as if a numb, listless passenger in a lofty, ornate ship's cabin, strapped securely to her chair by restraints of illness, as the room sailed through the haggard, sentinel oaks that guarded the angled Victorian roofs outside the window. "The Vicarage," they called the frowning, judgmental building that dominated the eastern ridge of the village. Its rambling porches wrapped its blue-green bulk with clutching white banisters, holding in and keeping out. High, haughty French doors had glared down East Jefferson Avenue with one accusing countenance or another as long as any living villager could remember. With effortless ostentation, it had presided through half a century, swept through the next, and now swaggered toward the starting edge of another.

The woman stared unblinking into the glaring morning beyond her window. Sharpened pencils and an open notebook arranged themselves in a symmetrical design on her lap. She thought heavily and with effort. Balance. Eternal, balanced truth. The Maker's rigid dictation, commanded and then left to find itself in the unfolding of Time. Failure to conform meant only grief and pain; apostasy would lead to endless remorse. Conformity, equally etched in struggle, laid paving stones on the path to eternal bliss. All must be in order, so far as could be seen by the world. The appearance of perfection demanded symmetry, balance. Appearance was everything.

Erratically, limping like wounded cats, other thoughts crept mirthlessly through her memory, stopping to curl up on that day in Florence when, as a young girl touring the Renaissance with her eyes and feeling its exuberance in her heart, she had dressed her emotions in the ever-flowering garments of romance, of classic perfectibility. She gave it no battle. She surrendered her body, mind, and soul to its beauty. She escaped into it.

She had decided from that unveiling moment that she would live as one being carved from pure marble. She would emerge at the end of her life to stand triumphantly amidst the heaps of useless, unwanted debris that had been chiseled from her by the Great Sculptor. She would endure the assaults of Devil and Man, repelling all. She would be purified by repentance through the sacrifice of the Savior. Then, unafraid to arrive as naked as Botticelli's Venus, anchored in the perfect shell of her baptism and totally beatific, she would stand before the Heavenly One. Finally, at His command, she would burst into the room that had been prepared for her from the beginning of Time and take her place in Perfection.

The brilliant, distant moment in the Italian city faded into the dusky sobriety of the round turret room. Filtering cataracts touched all she saw with a worn, yellow-dipped brush. The table beside her was stacked with books of various size and thickness, each in its place, all in prim order. All appeared leashed, restrained, as whispers about to be voiced. Some sure purpose seemed just ahead. But nothing was happening. There was no external movement to be seen, no activity to send the arrangement of person, room, and materials into a connected function. All was leaning, hanging, waiting for an expected signal, a breath, a command to enter a new moment.

Her body suddenly twitched, then stiffened. From a dark, festering corner of the woman's mind flew a fury of motion. Raging, roaring thoughts careened randomly and undisciplined through her awareness of herself; winged monsters hurtled and dove into her past and out again, battering her soul with a force powerful enough to destroy the entire village that lay below.

Trembling, she grasped the notebook and pencils, squeezing them with the icy pain of nubbed, arthritic fingers. Her dull, musty sight scratched desperately at the wavy old glass of the window, seeking a way through it, craving another world beyond its surface.

Then, freed by her imagination, visions sprang from her memory, pierced the window, and plunged beyond it, into her past. Released from all restrictions of her moment, she rushed madly down the hill and across its foot of rusty railroad tracks. She felt a surge of hot, angry judgment infuse her, propel her. Her thoughts probed and slashed along the sloping street like a blunted, mutilating surgeon's knife. At last she stopped, her gaze fixed upon the buildings which crowded that dreadful corner — Broad Street and East Jefferson Avenue.

It was all there, unchanged. Yes, that was the problem. Chaos! Unredeemed chaos! Unchanged! The iron picket fence around the courthouse lawn claimed one corner, its black and rust spikes dumbly gripping the scraggly lawn and caressing its daily collection of bent and broken plastic and aluminum litter. She shuddered at the thought of filthy trash falling like mindless sin from the grimy hands of the careless, mannerless hill-country peasants.

They would never change, though the wrath of God smote them with Eternal Justice! Coarse, repulsive gluttons! Slothful and ignorant descendants of cove dwellers and mill workers, they were no better than their savage, incest-crazed parents! Infested with myopic, diseased souls, they stumbled mindlessly through their wasteful lives of recurrent crisis and crime. Gorging on habit and lust, they reveled in violence and sin, unaware that they could claim a sublime heritage that was rooted in the chaste cottages and pious households of civilized England and Scotland.

Across the street from the courthouse, she knew, was Jameson's Family Pharmacy, crass and rude with its "new look" of aluminum and glass. Inside, the lunch counter was gone, and instead of delicious malts and fresh pimiento-cheese sandwiches there were greeting cards, computer supplies, fax machines and copiers for sale — along with several lines of winsomely packaged artificial herbs and wild-claiming health foods. Will Jameson ran the business, the third Jameson to hold title as the village pharmacist.

God willing he would be the last. His grandfather and father must be dying again in their graves, helpless to rescue their legacy from such defilement.

On another corner the tumbled rubble of Ray's Clothier lay disordered and scattered. Three years had passed since fire had struck the town's only clothing store, and nothing had been rebuilt. No one could say for sure that it was arson, but whispers linked the midnight blaze to Ray's decision to run for County Commissioner against "John John" Carpenter. The campaign had spawned a vicious and dirty fight. Even the big-city papers got into it after Ray alleged that widespread fraud and other hanky-panky had contaminated the commissioner's reign. Ray lost the race by a handful of votes, but shortly after the election investigators discovered that "John John's" good-old-boy style of management had allowed nearly a million dollars to be siphoned from the county roads budget over a period of six years.

Director of Roads Harold Spange was quickly indicted. The trial kept the county awake and entertained for several months, but ended in a mysterious haze of misplaced or lost records and an endless maze of conflicting lines of responsibility. Within a month of the court's dismissal, Ray's Clothier burned to the ground. "Regretfully," according to the county newspaper's account, the voluntary fire department was not notified in time to save the business. Whispers swept the town, shaped into rumors by the fact that the fire happened on the very day and at the very hour of a drunken party "John John" was hosting in honor of the volunteer fire department. By the time firefighters could stumble from the Commissioner's gracious farmhouse eight miles from the village and get organized, the building and its contents were heaps of glowing coals.

But all those thoughts were fleeting, merely framing the woman's fierce attention upon the remaining corner. She knew that a low, two-story building, ugly, scarred, and misshapen, lay sprawled and exhausted along Broad Street, then bent lethargically onto West Jefferson Avenue. It gawked vacantly up the hill of East Jefferson Avenue, helplessly mourning itself, a monument to those who held no values and had chosen despair and dereliction over the Good Life of Faith. Clinging desperately to the sidewalks that were as cracked as its own foundation, it wept with the angry sobs of the poor and struggling. To the woman, its façade was as patched, faded, and stained as its demonized residents.

At one time, when passenger trains were running twice a day between the state's major cities, the building had housed Harrison's Depot Hotel — the only hotel in the county. Mark Harrison's grandfather had hauled its bricks from four counties away, and had planed good, seasoned pine from nearby Hurlbut's Ridge for the frame and trim. It was built to last long enough to become old, nasty, and cantankerous.

Spanning three generations, its life cycle now entered the last gasping phase of its fourth generation. The woman repeated her refrain of judgment to herself. It had become a slum, she accused: no more than a resting place for rodent malingerers, welfare leeches, and the dregs of county life. Mark had been the village mayor for years, and saw to it that his building was "grandfathered in" under the new zoning ordinance imposed by the Twin Valley Authority. The blight remained. Nothing could purge her thoughts of it. The woman's eyes twitched in disgust as if stung by poisonous insects. It would continue to be the palace of human failure, a museum filled with willful human imperfection!

Her mind flashed with aversion, and blinding recognition exploded into her thoughts. She knew the woman was there! The fallen Queen of Sin! Suddenly tipping forward as if about to spring through the high turret window and fly witchlike above the oaks and descend upon the shabby building, the woman fixed her being upon the second-story window on the corner. She blinked her eyes. She must clear her eyes! She must pierce the space strung

between the elegant red, blue, and yellow rectangles that surrounded the dignified, clear pane of her window and the rotting,
scaling frame of the window in the old hotel. She must see it all
again! As always, the window would be open in warm weather
— and it would be filled with the disgusting, obese torso and
round-ball head of what was left of a woman.

It was Angel May MacDougald — or the bloated remnant
bearing her name! She leaned so far out of the window that her
balloonlike breasts flopped over the sill, pulsating to the rhythm
of her waving, pudgy arms. She wore no brassiere, and her faded
cotton dress was so scanty and thin that she could have worn
nothing for all that it covered. Pointing this way and that, mouth
alive with words beyond hearing, calling out to stranger and friend,
throwing her wispy-haired head back in cackling laughter, she
spent her days filling the air with meaningless banter and chit-
chat. She was incessantly alive with the compulsive, destructive
activity of a termite.

Insect! Vermin! Sloth! Wasted life! Willful choice of damna-
tion! The woman shuddered and closed her eyes. The notebook
and pencils slipped to the floor. She ignored them, grasping the
arms of the chair as if to save herself from falling. Opening her
eyes, she stared out the window, then squinted as if searching the
sky for something expected, perhaps a message from heaven, or
a gift of power to withstand the assault of the Devil.

Her lips of thin, purple ribbons moved slowly, mouthing a
deliberate, precisely formed prayer. As she looked heavenward
she saw what she thought might be the answer to her prayer,
what could be a sign from the Almighty! The ominous, dark wall
of a storm cloud began to fall from Frazier's Ridge and plunge
toward the northwest corner of the village. God's sign! Judgment!
Now!

Lightning and thunder filled the valley and cowed the ridges.
Then sudden winds hurled flushing sheets of rain against buildings

and through the village streets. The grasses of the well-kept lawns of the ridgeside homes clutched their thin layer of soil, bent in terror before the uncontrollable power of flooding storm water. The animated clutter and trash of the Broad Street gutters frolicked joyously, celebrating their deliverance from bondage into the unrestrained freedom of rushing water, dancing wildly in their chaotic journey toward grinning sewer mouths.

Angel May MacDougald felt the sudden wet wind, told the man she was flirting with that he'd better haul ass or get drowned, and hastily started to close her window. She shoved and jiggled it back and forth, finally slamming her shoulder against its sides when it refused to respond to her aggravated pushing and pulling. The coursing rain was already whipping loudly up and down Broad Street, careless of direction but convinced of its authority.

Finally, having wrestled the window as far down as it would go, Angel May turned heavily away into the little room and took the few shuffling steps needed to reach the stained sink on the opposite wall. Wadded in a damp clump beside the sink lay a dingy towel. She picked it up, rubbed it over her wet arms, and swept it around her neck and shoulders. The sweat and rain merged, then spread in a moist film over her. Her shoulders heaved as breath fought its way in and out. She felt chilled.

She had not heard there would be rain. Unexpected as all change, she thought. Made no difference, of course. Made no difference in a day, a week, an eternity — rain or no rain. Yearned for or unexpected. All was the same. The years came like the rain, sometimes in a drizzle, more often in a violent storm. She had forgotten whether to wish for it or dread its coming.

With a sigh that tapered into a low moan, she spread herself into an old stuffed chair that had once been a recliner. Now the handle at its side was missing, its stuffing oozed through worn spots, and its air of defiance dashed all hope for comfort. Clasping her hands upon her broad belly and closing her eyes, she listened to the rustling sound of the rain as it struck the roof above her. She said to no one: I must wait for the rain to stop. Oh, yes. I must wait for the rain to stop.

Earlier, before the morning people began to pass beneath her open window, she had been sitting there in the dawning's coolness, looking up East Jefferson Street, looking hard at The Vicarage. She had been thinking of Margaret Elizabeth Reeves, "Sissie" Reeves. Her Sissie. And of Sissie's father. She remembered those days when she and Sissie first met at school. She was a cove girl and Sissie was a ridge girl, but they touched one another with a magical friendship from the first day that they met. When recess came or any assignment was given that allowed them to be together, they sought each other, holding fast to the strange, stirring spirit that bonded them.

Sissie's father, the Reverend Jason James Reeves, Jr., was the pastor of two mountain missions in the county. He had grown up in the well-known Vicarage, for his father labored in this very ridgeland "vineyard" before him. The parson father had sent his son off to a church-related college, where the studious young Reeves discovered the same Jesus of the social gospel who had inspired his father's ministry.

After graduating from college, the son entered seminary. On a snowy winter's night at evening prayer, tears filled his eyes as he chanted the Magnificat, and he seemed to be kneeling beside the Virgin Mary and to understand her desire to obey God's command, regardless of the cost. He vowed to the God of the somber, stern rafters of the little seminary chapel, and to the Spirit symbolized by the uneven candles glowing grimly on the altar's retable, that he would forswear the temptations of the opulent city ministries for the self-imposed exile of service to the benighted souls of the ridgeland. One day he would return to his father's village. He would become God's agent for the salvation of the "poor and neglected folk" of his Prayer Book's prayers.

Following a successful curacy in the city and news of his father's approaching blindness and early retirement, he had indeed returned to his boyhood home. He had become the master of the Vicarage, of St. Peter's-in-the-hills and St. Mary's-in-the-valley, of his childhood sweetheart Wilma Jane Evans — and her considerable fortune in timberland and valley cotton — and, in time, of one child, Margaret Elizabeth, his forever-pure Sissie.

God had seemed to bless the days of the Reeves family — until Sissie first asked to bring home a new friend she had met at school. When she learned the friend was a "cove girl," Wilma Jane warned against it. But Father Reeves was in an evangelistic mood, and gave his permission. He usually found it difficult to reach the villagers, and thought Sissie's friend might provide the opportunity he had been looking for. Perhaps this would give him a way to break through the barriers of social class and worldly goods that frustrated his missionary outreach to "the other side of the tracks."

Angel May MacDougald came for her first after-school visit on a spring day during Eastertide. Her hair was wildly red, and her green-blue eyes were ever in a mode of feast and festival. A primordial energy seemed to erupt from deep within her, fusing her developing body into a vigorous harmony, causing her to move with the great strength and effortlessness of a gliding hawk. That same unleashing of hidden genes fueled her mind with the prowling, quick-moving curiosity of a famished fox.

Angel soon became the image of Father Reeves's dream. Through her he could begin to bring reform and new life in Christ to the fallen valley and cove people of the ridgelands. Her heart-wrenching life's story was to be given a happy ending by the miracles of redemption and salvation. Her father was unknown, though some said he was a man of "family" who might still be living in the village. Her mother sometimes worked as a maid to lower-middle-class villagers. But she was better known as the Broad Street whore! Perfect imperfection!

First after school, then on weekends, and then during the languid, syrupy summers, Angel became Sissie's beloved and sisterly companion. It was soon apparent that the parson began to view her as the favorite sister. Led by the spirited Father Reeves, Angel plunged into his library like an invading hunter, seeking and subduing intellectual prey of every kind. The mission-minded priest soon found that the only wit as sharp as his, the only grasp of ideas as firm as his, and the only appreciation of religious and secular literature as enthusiastic as his came from the one he called "my foster daughter."

Once, when it was Angel's turn to read from Tennyson's *Idylls of the King,* he was deeply moved when she burst into tears as she came upon Sweet Elaine's death from despair over her futile, unrequited love for Sir Lancelot. Angel's voice became Sweet Elaine's as she read the poor lady's letter with its death wish. Composing herself with great effort, she recited:

> "She grew so cheerful that they deemed her death
> Was rather in the fantasy than in the blood.
> But ten slow mornings past, and on the eleventh
> Her father lay the letter in her hand,
> And closed the hand upon it, and she died.
> So that day there was dole in Astolat."

And then Angel could read no more, and the tall cleric bent over her and put his arm about her as she cried without shame or restraint. The starch-smelling white collar at his throat brushed her wet cheek, and for an instant she had father and lover surrounding her, coming to her as a knight of the Table Round, slaying the harsh rejection and conquering the agonizing loneliness of her past, making her whole with his tender rescue. Father Reeves then brought Sissie into his embrace as well, and they all sobbed together until there were no more tears to flow, and silence parted them.

As Angel's brilliant and passionate intellectual, spiritual, and social light shone brighter and brighter, the modest, quiet, and comparatively dainty flame of interior light that burned within Sissie's soul sought ever deeper and more hidden regions for its flickering. When Father Reeves decided the girls and other members of their confirmation class were sufficiently prepared in the Catechism, he presented them to the bishop for confirmation. As the bishop questioned the anxious adolescents over their knowledge of the Church, it was Angel whose perfect, animated answers and strong convictions led the prelate to announce that all had done well. He later told Father Reeves that when his hands fell on Angel's glossy red head at confirmation he could feel a divine surge of grace flow through him into her.

The rain poured on, making memory difficult for Angel. Years of exasperated, hard drinking of whatever alcohol was at hand had blurred the past and made the present ever arrive as a surprise. Sluggishly and with considerable effort at first, she recalled those days at the Vicarage, locating them in random episodes that sulked in hazy corners of her mind, or discovering them as dusty collections of beautifully crafted artifacts that perched upon the neglected shelves of her experience. She seemed to be wandering about in a dimly lit cave. Searching for something. Afraid of finding it.

She opened her eyes. There was nothing on the other side of the window but the gray shade of rain. The Vicarage was up there, yes. Always there. In it was the gentle and yielding Sissie. In it was the memory of another rain, but one of awesome tears, of the rain that had washed her life away in an afternoon.

Closing her eyes again, she felt that frightening, dim afternoon creep through her body and form a vision in her mind. A summer storm had been raging through the village, flying swiftly from the northwest, twisting and turning without remorse. She had held Sissie so close, there in the turret room, high above the village, cheek pressed to cheek, bodies clinging heatedly together as they looked through the beautiful old window and down the sloping path of East Jefferson Avenue. Everything seemed awash in cleansing grace. The royal, ancient oaks bent and bowed as scepters of lightning cowed them with the power of Creation Day. Stimulated by the storm's reckless passion, their lips brushed together in dizzy excitement and affection.

Transformed, they felt their spirits snatched up by the wind. They floated beyond the village, the county, and the earth. As she held Sissie, protecting her from all the sharp, cutting edges of reality, from the Broad Street world she had come to loathe, Angel felt the flow of love washing over them like billowing blankets of moist, regenerating clouds. Peace, a welcome peace, turned all loneliness and all tempest into a kind, unexpected embrace.

And then Father Reeves opened the door, discovering the lovers. Angel's memory blackened. She tried to pull herself out of her chair, then fell back, trembling and weak. Her eyelids fluttered as spasms of fear shook her body. Was she awake or asleep? Where was she? Was she real? Did she exist any moment beyond that instant of final, brutal discovery? For a long time she sat there, motionless, senseless as a fat, hideous, dead toad. There was nothing for her to be. She was gone. She had disappeared into the thunder and lightning of the storm that would never end, would not give way to the sunlight of a new day. She quivered, breathless, and unredeemed.

Then, as if struggling to find life again, she stirred, opened her eyes, and shrieked, as with a practiced rocking motion she raised her great heft from the chair. Swaying toward the window, she heaved it open to the moist, cool air that followed the storm. She reached her hand out into the fresh newness, touching the moment of silence that separates the fearful hiding from a storm from the timid emergence into next things. She thought: Is it over? Oh, is it over at last?

Peering through the lingering mists, Angel looked up East Jefferson Avenue to the Vicarage. She thought of the day she heard that Sissie had been sent away to school where she would be living with an aunt. Later, she remembered placing the news that Sissie was going to school in Switzerland against her breast like a knife. Each step sent her friend farther away, bringing undiluted loneliness closer and closer.

She knew that she could never go back to the mysterious and awe-inspiring shelter of St. Mary's-in-the-valley. It had become for her a catacomb, a burial place for God's love and human hope. Father Reeves's rage had spread through the entire congregation and spilled into the mouths of the just. From the chancels of their spacious ridgetop homes they had murmured in antiphonal agreement: "After all we have done for the little waif!" When they had properly offered their litanies of disgust, they gratefully committed her soul to God without further interference from them.

Overcome with shame and dismay, Angel had anxiously struggled to grasp and accept the sudden, unfeeling sentence of exile. Nothing she did could bring either understanding or hope. She knew that she must return to the Broad Street culture "where she belonged." But she could not hold back the militant depression, anger, and fierce loneliness that she felt. Her sense of being loved for herself lay crumpled like the unwanted, discarded trash that clogged the gutters of the village streets. She lost all sense of having control over her life. Slowly drained of her energy and power, believing herself worthless and discarded, she slipped from the world and into the cavern of her despair.

And she knew she would never share Sissie's life again. As the years wept through her, and she wept through the years, she followed the way of her mother. In unrewarding searches without number, she tried to find closeness to men or women. Always there was nothing at the end of the search but its finality, its failure to bring a future with it, its verdict of illusion. Emptiness swelled like a permanent night of loneliness around her, and in its center she made her bed.

In recent years she had used her welfare check and what remained of her body to rent the little room in the old hotel. When she was not teasing and shouting with the passers-by, she was sitting in her chair or leaning out the window, watching the lovely, turret window of the Vicarage as it gazed upon the village like a blind, Cyclopean eye. And she wondered what Sissie might be doing at that moment. Always she wondered.

Now, as she watched the laggard streams of storm-water trickle down the gutters from the ridge above the Vicarage, she became aware that an ambulance had swerved from Broad Street to climb noisily up East Jefferson Avenue. When it reached the Vicarage, it turned crisply into its driveway and disappeared. Angel blinked, then stared, then recoiled a step from the window as if roughly pushed by a hostile force pouring from the Vicarage. Time hung in her heart, suspended on the shattered remnants of her memory of love, real love, the only love she had ever known. And then the ambulance, quietly and without alarm or lights, pulled listlessly out of the driveway and joined the last trickles of the storm on the way to Broad Street. Bumping across the railroad tracks, it turned under her window and joined the Broad Street traffic that had been waiting for the storm's ending sighs before starting its normal hum of life again. Oh, Angel thought. Oh, the storm, the storm! And she turned from the window into the growing shadows of her room.

After a while, she did not know how much later, she returned to the window. Evening was filling the village streets with remorse from the stormy day. Angel shouted at the first person to walk beneath her window, a friend who worked at the supermarket down the street. What was the ruckus up at The Vicarage? Seems they found Miss Margaret Elizabeth Reeves dead, sitting up there in that steeple thing on the house. They say she was looking out the window and just sitting there with her eyes wide open. Dead as dead. Might have taken too much of something, they say.

Angel thanked him and pulled herself from the window and back into the room. She stood for a moment, like a grotesque, ridiculous mockery of Renaissance perfection. Then she shuffled about, aimlessly pushing her few belongings into little disorderly piles, then nervously picking and searching through each one. She seemed to be looking for something she could not find.

Again, she stood for a while, frozen in the midst of something she could not quite recall. Moving slowly again, she appeared to have abandoned the search, now unsure what it was that had eluded her. She returned to the window, fought it closed, pulled down the ragged shade and rolled heavily onto the narrow, disheveled bed that stretched the length of one wall. Lying on her back, she closed her eyes and tried to find a path toward beauty on the map of ugly rejection that unfolded from her soul into her mind. Tears began to puddle in the cups of her eyes, and she sighed the gentle sound that marks the end of a storm. It had been a terrible storm, she thought, and had lasted, but for one brief interlude, throughout her lifetime.

In a sheltered corner of the room's dark and messy floor lay a yellowed newspaper clipping featuring a large picture of "The Rev. Fr. Jason James Reeves, Jr." Beneath the picture flowed a wordy obituary of some length, extolling his life of service to the downtrodden and needy in the county. The parson's eyes were focused straight ahead, his lips pursed, unsmiling. His round, white clerical collar wrapped his long neck with the symbol of purity and perfection.

Near her father's picture, much smaller and barely noticeable, lay a childhood school photo of Sissie Reeves, smiling her shy smile and looking straight ahead as if expecting a loving word from a friend. Both pictures had escaped Angel's search, had fallen from the accidental and meaningless confusion that decorated the room in hopelessness.

Then, as the dark room held her thoughts safely in its arms, Angel began to chant softly in a voice from youth and happy times, a voice that slowly became more clear, even, and sure. Her memory became strong, and she felt confident and unafraid. She became aware that others were joining her in her song: sweet Elaine, her dear Sissie, and the kindly Father Reeves. As they held one another they sang again the ancient words from *Idylls of the King,* the Song of Love and Death:

> "Sweet is true love tho' given in vain, in vain;
> And sweet is death who puts an end to pain:
> I know not which is sweeter, no not I.
> I fain would follow love, if that could be;
> I needs must follow death, who calls for me;
> Call and I follow, I follow! Let me die."

Quietly, with a touch of reverence, the night drew the shroud of darkness over the little village. East Jefferson Avenue lay hushed in serene ebony, noiselessly becoming its next age. At the top of the street, a graceful Victorian window whispered sadly through the restraint of its elegant draperies of old brocade. At the foot of the ridge a battered and weary window sighed in relief behind a tattered shade.

I opened my eyes. Only silence of the story's end sat beside me on the porch. Getting up from my chair, I fumbled for the doorknob I knew must be there, turned it slowly, and entered the pitch-black cottage. I reached for the light switch, then pulled my hand away. Drifting through the night, from a far-distant place, came the long, moaning whistle of a train. Then, nothing more.

Zack and the Little King

We had already played twelve holes, "bets as usual," when Zack began to tell stories. He promised he would tell me about the Little King. I needed something to cheer me up. Zack's drive hit the canted bend in the exact middle of the thirteenth fairway and pertly disappeared around the dogleg to the right. Mine stayed to the right and short of the bend, scurrying with disobedient arrogance to the edge of the rough, resting with impossible lie in the mocking scruff.

It had been this way for six out of twelve. I didn't need to check my scorecard to know I owed the guy thirty dollars and counting. "Why do you go on playing with him?" I kept asking myself.

I guess the answer is that this is the kind of humiliation that suits me. It's worth the whipping I take just to hear him talk, to listen to his stories. And I am a sucker for stories.

At eighty, Zack is almost twenty years older than I, and he is also longer off the tee and sharper on the green than all but a handful of the other members of the club. His felt cap has dog hairs on it, and his "lucky" sweater usually advertises his morning egg, unless Lily, his ageless and charming wife, catches him on the way out the house.

But his game is impeccable, neat, clean. And his stories are like his game. They soar majestically, like a perfect tee shot, and they wax and wane with the ups and downs of life before they find their ending in the cup on the green (and they always do just that).

Zack Fulbright is six-four, straight as a Greek temple column, and jammed full of a lifetime of rare experiences. Reared in the rugged Blue Ridge foothills, he and his brother learned early to shoot and fish and run their own lives. Maybe it was something in the water that made them as hardheaded as the field stones they toted to make room for their daddy to plant his corn. Perhaps there is something in the lavish southern air that freed their spirits and convinced them that they could see nearly to the ends of the earth.

While still a youngster, Zack became the "fixer" for the whole county, showing a genius for working with machinery, improvising to salvage scarce and precious equipment when it was ailing. When he left home at fifteen to work in one of the glowering red-brick cotton mills in a nearby town, he was already an imposing ramrod of a man. His mind and body flexed to the same tune, and before he was twenty he had concluded that the world was just the right size for him to romp in. Even then, he suspected that its borders might need to be pushed out a bit, and that he would have little difficulty with the task. He set about living an audaciously exuberant life composed of stories — magical stories laid end on end, stretching around the globe.

He had a short approach and a shaky chip shot, but sank a rolling 20-foot putt for a birdie four. I nicked a limb trying to cut the corner to the green, lifted a fine five iron not too far from the pin, and two-putted for my par. As usual, not good enough. I was seven down. Thirty-five dollars down and counting. Zack started telling stories. Blessed relief.

He said that he had known the great golfer, Woodrow "Woody" Winston. Even played a lot of golf with him. By that time Winston was past his prime and beginning to be affected by his final illness. Nevertheless, the great golfer took a shine to the tall, lithe, and graceful Zack, spent considerable playing time with him, and gave him valuable pointers to improve his game. He even told Zack that he should get out of the manufacturing business and become a professional golfer. Zack gave it plenty of thought. He knew he had talent. And he swears that his putting became deadly accurate after he watched Woody gently flick his famous putter, "Sweet Tomorrow," across the short grass of the green.

But Zack was already winning on another course. By that time he was a rising star in an industry that was growing at the exhilarating pace that suited him. Coming to be known as the best young production engineer in the business, he was attracting wide attention, his specialty being the design of new mills and modification of existing ones.

He did not forget golf. It had become his sport of choice, played earnestly and competitively when he had time. But his boyhood skills remained. When he could, he continued to go hunting during the various seasons, stalking deer in the Deep South's piney woods, picking wild turkeys off rugged mountainsides, and taking his limit of doves and quail from their broad broomsedge fields.

Zack told of a day when he was playing with Woody when the famed golfer had a weak spell, stopped, waved the following foursome through, and shared confidentially with him how tough it was to begin to be slowed down by illness. He knew he would not be able to play much longer. Then, with a faint twinkle in his eye, he said, "Zack, being sick like this is like being in a sand trap on the edge of the green, thirty feet from the pin, with a five-foot overhang in the way."

He paused, pulled a five iron out of his bag for his next shot, and continued wistfully. "Then you look over to your bag and find the only club you have is a driver. Look as you may for a sand wedge, there's only a driver to get you out of the trap."

Zack thought a minute, pulled his driver from his bag, looked at it from several angles, and said, "Well, Woody, I guess we'll just have to figure out something new — like, how to get out of sand traps using a driver." That's how Zack saw the world of sand traps, and how he approached any other obstacles in his way. And that was why Winston and all others Zack met liked and had confidence in the man.

By the time we had finished eighteen and I had paid Zack the forty bucks I had lost (and he had said thanks for the contribution to his favorite charity — an inner-city home for wayward children), he was well into another story that flowed seamlessly into our dinner at the Nineteenth Hole Restaurant. It was the astonishing account of his friendship with the famous king of an exotic foreign country half a world away. Zack called him the "Little King."

It seems that Zack was working for an international company that had built a large plant in the King's developing country. Zack had helped set up the project but had never met the monarch. Now it appeared that the plant was losing money disastrously, and the monarch and his cronies were already $27 million behind in scheduled payments to Zack's company. No one had been able to get an audience with the Little King in order to persuade him to come up with the money. The officials at his plant avoided every attempt at consultation or intervention.

The president, chief executive officer, and board members of Zack's company met to "pray" over the problem. The answer to their prayers, they concluded, was Zachariah Amos Fulbright. They called Zack in and announced that their decision was unanimous — he was the man to go out there and put things right. They told him that he was the best they had at dealing with all kinds of people. While they were chattering away, Zack was mirthfully predicting how his flatterers would react when he accepted — and told them he would do it for ten percent of the money he recovered.

In a week he was away, first class, in the wake of his terse telegram to the Little King declaring that he needed to see him immediately on urgent matters of business. When Zack arrived at the capital, he was wearing a black silk suit with a white cotton, wide-collared shirt, carelessly open at the neck. He stood aloof from the clamor of the Customs Office and the dirty bedlam of his surroundings. His great height and noble bearing marked him as a foreigner of great importance. The air terminal manager appeared, apologized for not knowing who he was, and wanted to know how he could be of help. Zack's answer was short and to the point: "I am Zachariah Amos Fulbright, and I have come to see your king."

At this point in the telling Zack departed from his tale to recollect a story he had heard from a preacher friend of his. It seems that a fool decided he should become his Emperor's wise man. As he traveled to the palace people asked him where he was going and why. He always answered that he was going to the palace to become the Emperor's wise man. Everyone laughed when they heard this, but the fool, undaunted, traveled on.

When he was brought before the Emperor, that august person asked why he had intruded upon his ceremonially busy day.

"I have come to be the Emperor's wise man," replied the fool.

The Emperor and his courtiers burst out laughing, and scoffed at the silly man standing before them. "What makes you think that you could be the Emperor's wise man?" asked the Emperor.

"Oho, it's very clear. Already you have begun to ask me important questions," responded the fool with gentle seriousness.

Stunned, the Emperor finally found his tongue. "Well, now, what do you suppose the people would say if they knew that their Emperor had a fool for his wise man?"

With affectionate patience, the fool replied, "It would be better to have a fool for a wise man than a fool for an emperor."

Caught in the fool's web, the Emperor stammered, "Now I am the one who feels like a fool!"

"Of course, that cannot be," counseled the fool, "for only a fool has never felt like one."

After the fool's last response, Zack laughed joyously at his little fable. I asked if I should conclude that he had been the fool who had been bold enough to visit the Emperor. He looked at me with twinkling eyes and said I would have to be the judge of that. And then he resumed the interrupted tale, taking me back to the bustling airport in the Little King's faraway land.

The air terminal manager smiled when Zack told him he had come to see the king. Zack did not smile. From his advantageous height, towering over the little manager by a good two feet, Zack handed him a $100 bill and coolly instructed him to see that his luggage was moved expeditiously through Customs and transported to his hotel. He then wheeled about and strode into the rotunda of the air terminal. A man in a chauffeur's uniform approached, bowed, and led him through the confusion toward the big Cadillac limousine Zack had ordered to meet him.

Before he could step outside the building, however, the air terminal manager came running and pushing after him. Pulling on Zack's arm, he announced in breathless disbelief, "The King will see you now! Please follow me, Sir!" He led Zack across the room, past a burly guard, and into a VIP suite off the rotunda. As they scurried along, the manager was explaining excitedly that the King had come to the airport to see his daughter off on a trip, learned of Zack's arrival, and demanded to see him at once.

There, in the relative quiet of the VIP suite, the two men met face to face.

"You are Zachariah Amos Fulbright," the diminutive monarch said in even tones, unintimidated by Zack's impressive height. "My advisers tell me they call you Zack. What shall I call you?"

"Zack, your majesty. Just Zack. And what shall I call you?" the tall, erect man inquired.

Zack's response seemed to delight the monarch, who did not know that Zack had already dubbed him the "Little King" in his mind. With a touch of royal humility, he responded, "One of my names is Samuel, a great man from the Bible. It would please me if you called me, simply, Sam."

"All right, Sam. I have come to help out if I can. I suppose you got my telegram. Where do we go from here?"

This unlikely pair went many places from there. The primary energy that motivated them was a growing trust in one another. From this emerged a fast friendship. The Little King was a delicate and sensitive mouse of a man, the American a gentle but assured giant. The two of them, whether dining at the palace or touring the mill, seemed to have endless ideas to bounce off one another and a world of stories to share.

Zack had crossed the border of a mere desire to pocket his fat fee for doing the job. He found that he had entered earnestly into the search for a way to help his friend — whom he called, as requested, just "Sam." The Little King sensed this, and their mutual trust grew daily. Zack got down to business.

Certain events soon gave Zack insights into the character of his host. Once, before a dinner meeting at the palace, Zack was introduced to a beautiful woman of the country who stood shyly beside the Little King. She was one of his daughters-in-law. Then two bright and attractive young children came running into the room to embrace their grandfather. The monarch explained sadly that the three were all that remained of the family of one of his sons, for the son had committed a serious offense, and the monarch had had to order his execution.

Seeing Zack's eyes open in surprise, he explained that, as the King, he expected utter honesty and openness from everyone, including his family. He carried the morals of his country on his shoulders, he said, for he had been chosen by God to be the King, and everyone in the land, including the ruling heads of the state religion, was subject to his wisdom and command. Zack got the point.

After the first two weeks Zack was beginning to think he might never grasp the problem at the mill. It had been set up to produce large quantities of various products needed in the region. He thought it strange that from the day of his arrival, it had been whirring noisily at full capacity. Trucks from every part of the region lined up at the shipping docks to load and carry the finished products away. It seemed to him ridiculous, even mysterious, that such a busy plant could be operating at such a tremendous loss. He surmised, uncomfortably, that some of the officials were playing loose with the money. A picture formed in his mind, with grotesque literal clarity, of heads beginning to fall.

On closer inspection and in time, however, he saw the true nature of the problem. He was relieved to find that the glitch lay outside the pockets of the managers. The reality was that the entire production capacity of the plant had been commandeered to produce rolls of toilet paper in a never-ending flow! Machinery designed to make other products lay idle, while tons of the white rolls surged off the production lines every day. Even so, production could not keep up with the demand.

He learned that the King's subjects and others beyond the little kingdom's borders were using the toilet paper for dashing white headbands, much-needed inexpensive bandages, decorations for their dwellings, barter items, and — hopefully — for its original purpose. Because the toilet paper was a low-profit item, insufficient revenues were being generated to cover the cost of production. The frantic strategy of the managers had been to increase production. It was not working. While some of the most valuable equipment in the mill stood idle, the Little King and his production managers remained baffled by the paradox of so much activity and no financial success.

It took a month and several personal appearances at the plant by the Little King to bring about the necessary changes. By cutting the production of toilet paper in half, then half again, and making use of the machinery already in place that could produce other high-profit items, the profit picture speedily turned around. But no sooner had the original problem been solved than another took its place.

This time it was a labor problem. For two years the production workers had been making the same product — toilet paper. They believed that they had become experts at their task, and they had become familiar with their routine assignments. Now, suddenly, they were thrust into the midst of change against their will. They became depressed, and their earlier enthusiasm for their work diminished until Zack estimated that they were working at seventy-five percent efficiency or less.

By this time Zack had set up a camp near the plant and the plant village, complete with kitchen and sleeping quarters for himself and the top managers. This had greatly facilitated the intense planning and implementation necessary to set things on the right course.

One morning Zack noticed that his cooks were making huge pans of macaroni-and-cheese, far too much for the few members of his staff to eat. Making inquiries, he discovered that the cooks craved this unusual food, were making extra portions for themselves, and were taking leftovers home with them. He then further observed that there were dozens of little children from the plant village always hanging around the kitchen, pestering the cooks for handouts.

He ordered the cooks to make extra macaroni-and-cheese and to give portions to the children. On the first morning the grubby children laughed at the gluey yellow stuff in the pans. On the second day the more adventurous ones stuck their fingers in it and tasted it, while the rest awaited their judgment. On the third day every child in the village and most of the women were on hand for the distribution of the macaroni-and-cheese. As Zack put it, "There was macaroni-mania everywhere!"

Then Zack had an idea. He called in some of the supervisors and told them he believed that eating quantities of macaroni-and-cheese would make them stronger, make them live longer, and bring happiness to their families. He offered to provide free macaroni-and-cheese for the plant village, adding that he expected to see great improvement in the workers' performance as a result.

Within a week the plant was operating at full efficiency, and nothing more was heard of the labor problem. Of course, Zack was faced with his own production problem: how to produce 200 pans of macaroni-and-cheese every day. He set up a new kitchen, flew in three-quarters of a ton of uncooked macaroni from the States, and kept the macaroni-and-cheese rolling out in rhythm with the mill's production.

Having at last put the plant into a solid profit state, Zack then told the Little King that he had to get back home to his family and friends. The Little King sadly agreed, inviting him to the palace for a farewell dinner. As they were toasting one another and swapping tall tales, a servant appeared and placed a silver platter before Zack. On the platter was a slim envelope. The monarch cheerfully commanded him to read the inscription on the ornate platter and then to open the envelope. Zack read:

> To His Honor Zachariah Amos "Zack" Fulbright
> Friend and Honorary Citizen of the Kingdom
> Wise Counselor and Teacher to the King
> With Sincere Thanks, "Sam"

When he opened the envelope, Zack found a check made out to his company for $27 million. The Little King accepted his thanks, leaned across the table toward him, and asked, "Zack, how much would it cost to build another mill half again the size of the one we have?"

Zack touched his forehead for a moment, then replied, "Sam, I don't see how you could do it for less than three million."

"Good!" exulted the Little King. "When can you start?"

"As soon as I get home, talk to the company, and have a nice, long vacation," Zack replied.

The Little King raised his glass. "You're on!" he exclaimed with obvious delight.

I asked Zack if that was the end of the story. We had finished our dinner some time before, and the waiters were letting us know that we were the last ones in the restaurant.

"Just about," he said, reaching into his pocket for a roll of bills to leave a tip and pay for our meal.

"Well, did you do it?"

He regarded me with surprise at such an absurd question. "Sure I did it!" he growled, with a contained trace of pique. "I gave Sam my word, and my word is as good as his. I've got the second tray beside the first on the mantelpiece at home. Come by and I'll show it to you!"

I did, and he did.

I still haven't asked him if he thought of himself as the fool in the fable. I might do that sometime. I guess it's worth losing a few dollars now and then to have a chance to play eighteen with Zack. I've encouraged him to get his life stories on tape. He agrees he ought to do it but doesn't seem to make any progress toward the task. Actually, he's too busy starting new stories to stop long enough to record the old ones.

I petitioned his wife, Lily, to intercede for me, to get him to record his life. She just laughed. "Me get Zack to do anything?

Well, I never really tried, but I don't think it would work any better than trying to slow him down. And besides, after fifty-five years of the most-fun marriage to that crazy giant, I'm not about to risk ruining it this late in life! After all, he's only eighty, and I have to keep running to stay up with him as it is."

I said I thought I understood. That same afternoon I put aside fifty bucks for his favorite charity and called Zack up to see when we could play another round.   ✹

The Carpenter

Today I fired the Carpenter. When his two sidekicks came by at midmorning to get their tools, I was waiting for them. I told them to pick up all of their tools and tell the Carpenter that I could not continue this way.

They acted like they had been down this road before. Young Mike obviously felt bad about it, looking at the floor and kicking at some stray boards at his feet as we talked. He asked me several times to tell him again just what to say when he got back to the Carpenter. I told him to tell the Carpenter that I was very disappointed that things didn't work out, and that in the spirit of Hemingway and Faulkner I would look deeper into the human situation — and "Thanks for much." Mike said he could remember the thanks part of the message.

But Mike understood. Not the Hemingway stuff, but the way things had not worked out. He had walked that path with the Carpenter before. The other lad — the new one — just grinned as if he had done something wrong but was not sure what it was or how it had happened.

But I was not thinking about "right" or "wrong." I was feeling that kind of disappointment that does not search for something anyone has done. Or not done. I felt that vague uneasiness that I feel when what I hoped for in a person or an event doesn't show up as scheduled by my expectations. The Carpenter and I had taken quite a trip beyond the Nature of Things as I usually viewed them. And now we had returned to the starting place. Or the ending place. They had become one. I'm still not sure just how I feel about it.

I guess I'm supposed to say that I "learned something" from it all. We're supposed to say something like that when we risk an adventure where everyone else says it's always been done another way, the same old way, and we try to put a new spin on it.

But, much as I hate to admit it, there are some things in some situations that simply need to be done or the situation will disappear, leaving you holding a garbage can full of frustrated desires, spoiled ambitions, and soured hopes. I had depended on the Carpenter for some of those primary elements of orderly support. Theories and philosophical observations don't hammer nails into boards. As I said, it didn't work out.

He was — and will continue to be — a special person to me. Not one of the herd, certainly. I interviewed six carpenters before I talked with him. He was my "lucky seven." It was clear that I could work best with him. The others said that they were not like other carpenters, and intoned a litany of others' sins. They made their profession appear to be populated with petty criminals who were bent on inflicting endless torments of psychological abuse upon unsuspecting customers.

And each said that he could do all the work necessary to remodel the building and get the place open for business on my schedule. Each said "no sweat" about turning the former savings and loan into a restaurant. My drawings, they all agreed, were "clear as a bell." And they all asked enthusiastically, "When do I start?" I was impressed that they all emphasized the same point — I could count on them. And they all righteously declared that I could not count on the others.

Each carpenter added his own unique sales pitch as he went through his ritual of self-promotion. Except the Carpenter. After looking at my sketches, he said quietly that he would do his best to see me through. But he said nothing of the others or of his profession. He seemed to exist at hovering distance above them, almost unaware of their earthiness, lost in contemplating his own being at the moment. He did not praise my sketches or pull his hammer from his belt, eager to begin. He did finger a book half-showing from his belt, as if he were thinking somewhere on a ladder between our conversation and it. The title read: *Slaughter-house-Five*. A carpenter who reads Vonnegut? What would it be like, I thought, to work with a carpenter who could hear the droning of Allied bombers over Dresden, who could wince at the cries of wounded and dying German civilians? I hired him on the spot.

I had only the summer to complete the transformation of the bank into a restaurant. The target was late August. I had to return to the university for faculty meetings by early September, and confidently promised my brother and his investors that I would bring the remodeling up to the finish line before that time. Then, if necessary, one of them could tidy it up and open. For my efforts I would add a much-needed bulge to my cramped university salary. I had done this for them twice before, and it seemed to work for all of us.

The Carpenter agreed that I would work under him as a "go-fer." I knew enough not to interfere, but knew enough to be of help. I soon learned that there would be more to it than that. I was to become his student, he was to become my master. Without course introduction or outline, I suddenly found myself in a well-directed laboratory of mysteries. He performed miracles — and then turned them into the commonplace by showing me that even I could demythologize the enchanted, unreachable ortho-doxies of his craft.

The Carpenter fit my idea of a collegial friend. A mentor. The kind of friend you make when you are being taught how to probe beyond the outer edge of your own perceptions. The one who lays wisdom like a carpet on the paths where there is none. He was that person for me. Literature and construction were com-panions, interchangeable at our whim.

Work was a joy when he and his little crew were there. From my "blueprints," with their primitive scaled-down lines, there began to emerge, even from the first day, the true shape of a restaurant. For several weeks a vague, shifting mist seeped into the spaces between the old bank's rigid configurations and the new restaurant's supple shapes. Then, in a splendid, unexpected moment of howling saws and thunderous hammering, the restaurant began to claim its own existence and to jauntily pull away from its past. I shouted my exuberance into the spray of sawdust and the smell of freshly incised lumber. It was happening! Birth! New life! A new creation! It was like writing an exciting new book composed of reality.

Our progress was obvious to all who walked past the building. The men who ran the businesses or worked in the office buildings up and down Main Street kept coming in like paternalistic inspectors, strolling through the chaos and announcing that "It sure looks good," and "You guys are doing a great job." They always asked, "When do you think you'll be open?" I introduced them all to the Carpenter. I said it was up to him. They could tell that I was proud to be working with him.

I chose the Carpenter to do the job because I sensed that I could communicate with him. When I said I wanted to preserve as much of the dancing, colorful marble and poised, rich-toned walnut from the old bank as possible, he understood exactly where the aesthetics of my wishes came from. He seemed to understand my visions, even when they were left to hang on the webs of my untutored descriptions and instructions. I reflected: How few, even among the faculty members at the university, truly listen to the meaning beneath words, or try to understand the visions that lie behind the fragments of another's language. The Carpenter was one of the few.

The Carpenter taught me many things. He knew so much about the city that I began to have a sense of belonging in this hot, steaming community over a hundred miles from my home. In a way divined only by oracles, he had come to know secrets about all of the old families. It didn't slow down the work, but amid the pounding and the shrieking of hammers and power saws, and without surgical judgments or petty elaboration, the cultural viscera of the city passed between us. Often, after the day's work, he would describe influential and notorious Main Street citizens as if they were unchanging figures, monuments to the history and lore of the city, and frozen in the packages of their reputations forever.

There were successes. Like the poor Greek who came to town years ago. Couldn't speak English beyond "Hello" and "Goodbye." No one would lend him a nickel. He worked as a janitor, saved his money, started a tiny greasy-spoon cafe, and now was a millionaire owner of steakhouses in three states. His original steakhouse was just around the corner and down by the riverwalk. Still packed every day except Sunday.

There was wild hysteria among the city's elite when he, "that greasy Greek," paid cash for one of the antebellum homes on "The Hill," the city's most distinguished old neighborhood. But his appearance of great wealth and his largesse in support of the local symphony eventually "absorbed" enough of his Greekness to ensure the survival of his kids and their kids in a community suspicious of strangers — and especially "foreigners."

The Carpenter told many tales about the families whose elegant homes stretched from one end of The Hill to the other. He explained in detail how they made money without working as regular people did. His stories were about clever bankruptcy schemes, lying and misrepresentation for gain, arranged — and profitable — marriages, slick land deals, corporate hoodwinks, and cashing in on "inside information" from crooked state and local politicians. I forget which ones were alcoholics or who had been caught in another city with someone's wife. But it was clear that about the only inhabitant of The Hill to gather a fortune honestly, and gain the approval of the Carpenter, was the Greek.

But, to the Carpenter's eye, there occasionally appeared an exceptional public figure who gave the city needed leadership and a positive image. Just across the street, he pointed out, was the law office of one of the state's greatest governors. Of course he had been dead for years, but his name was still there in gold and black letters, kept fresh by those in the firm who survived in his shadow.

When "Old South" governors were trying to preserve racism in the embalming fluids of segregation, this governor saw into the future. He had led the state past its dependence upon a hundred years of trite Civil War slogans and into a new way of looking at things. In the spirit of the times, of course, there were some business leaders on Main Street and some families on The Hill who never spoke to the governor or his family again. Although he did not mention the fact to me, I had already noticed that the Carpenter's crew was half African-American and half White, and that he treated each worker with the same firm respect.

To my surprise, the Carpenter kept up with the stock market. I could never tell if he was into the game, but it was clear that he considered anyone who "didn't keep up with the Dow" to be a bit undereducated, possibly unaware of the significance of what he called the "temple of American religious faith" — the New York Stock Exchange. He seemed to know the holdings of most of the richest citizens in town, and claimed that sufficient shares of some international corporations were owned by people on The Hill to change drink formulas and automobile designs.

On several occasions we talked about religion. The Carpenter and his wife had joined a philosophical movement a few years before. They saw little use in any of the organized religions, especially the Christian variety. He explained to me in detail how carefully he avoided anyone who said that God told them what to do. They could not be trusted as far as you could throw their churches. He did not know where he had read it, but he agreed with someone who wrote that people went to church to "fool God," and then lived their lives as if God did not exist. I asked if it might have been the Danish theologian, Kierkegaard. He smiled and asked me to pronounce that man's name again. Yes, that may be who it was, he said, but he didn't know just how to pronounce it. His philosophical study group had discussed some of Kierkegaard's thoughts.

He and his wife were stimulated as well by some "Eastern teachings," he said. They liked what they knew of Taoism and Hinduism. He said those traditions seemed anxious to free themselves from dishonesty and immorality — from the demands of the world of cruelty and violence. He wondered what would happen if people stopped trying to outdo one another, but, instead, worked together for the common good. He was thinking about trying out those strange teachings about eating only vegetables, but hadn't decided about that yet.

For him, most politicians were the worst breed of humankind. He reminded me that Aristotle or some philosopher had once said that human beings are political animals. That was an accusation and not a tribute, as far as he could tell. He was sure that people had been taught to want money and power more than to want to do a good job or to do good things for others. This made him sad on some days. On others he was angry about it. He was furious with the Allies for their slaughter-bombings of the civilians of Dresden and other German cities. Retaliation for German atrocities was no excuse, and merely weakened the moral position of those who retaliated. Reading Vonnegut's book had increased his revulsion to war. When you can shovel a whole city into a heap of rubble the size of a small mountain, he grumbled, you have only the politicians and their big-profit war machines to thank for it.

In the meantime, while we were sharing our lives with one another, the restaurant was being artfully sculpted and was nearing completion. There remained just a few crucial weeks of detail, painting, and floor finishing. Soon signs announcing the opening would spread across the windows. It would be the most attractive and best-designed restaurant in my brother's chain. I could hardly wait to throw open the doors and show the city what a really good restaurant was like.

And then, one Monday morning, after I had driven the three hours from a weekend visit home to meet the Carpenter and crew at our usual 8:30-ish starting time, I found myself alone in the silent restaurant, waiting. They did not show up all morning. Or all day. The Carpenter did not call. Was he sick? Had there been an accident? Had there been a misunderstanding? I tried to call him, every number I could think of. No answer.

I began to know how it was. As the day wore on I swore and paced about the place, searching for an emotion that would not destroy me. Some of his tools were still in the corner where he had left them on Saturday afternoon. He would explain, I knew, and be back the next day. Think positive. Don't think.

He was, after all, just a carpenter, I reminded myself almost laughingly. And carpenters do that. They say they will be someplace at a certain time and they do not come. Like misplacing marriage vows and neglecting political promises, they say one thing and do another. Some get drunk or something crazy happens. The Carpenter did not drink and was the most sane man I had met in years. What was wrong?

Could it be that my Carpenter was, and would always be, a man of his profession? Just a man of his profession? I knew that carpenters often get involved in several jobs at once. University professors do that, too. Then they begin to live like deer in a forest fire, running from one commitment to another and through the anxiety and terror of consuming impossibilities. They must dash madly everywhere, from one island of safety to the next. They begin to become as other men.

When a carpenter begins to pull clever tricks, create sumptuous lies, and forget to be patient; when he starts to confuse his memory of one job with the anticipation of another; then he becomes wily and a master at trickery and deceit. He has lured the players of his choice into his own dangerous game, and feels compelled to rankle the puzzle with irritants of cunning.

Others must chase him, find his lair. Cornered or not, he becomes defensive and hostile. He blames the weather, his suppliers, his helpers, his family — anyone and anything! He tries to survive in the world he wishes he could stand above and control with his expertise and prophecies. He shudders. He knows he has become another of those who scramble the network of lies and tricks to maintain their allotted place, to establish their right to be. The goal has become survival. That is all.

I drove across the river to our twin town at 7:30 a.m. I had not seen the Carpenter or any of his crew for two days. No phones were being answered. If the restaurant is to open on schedule, I thought, I must find him. It was nearing the crucial date for his return to the job. There was not much time left. The morning was cloudy, stuffy, oppressive. I felt it in my chest. I had heard a rumor that he was working a new job near a shopping center across the river. I would try to find him.

I found his truck parked in front of a rubble-filled building and pulled into the space beside it. No one was inside the truck or the building. The men working in the next building had not seen him. One man thought he had left the truck the night before, and would arrive shortly after picking up some of his crew. Yesterday they started work about 8:30, he said.

I waited. In half an hour he drove up, his old Oldsmobile crammed with his crew. He was short with me, looked past me when we talked, but agreed to come over to my restaurant later in the day. He could work this evening and then start tomorrow to finish up, he said. I told him that some of his tools were still there in the corner where he had left them. He looked surprised, as if just remembering something that bothered him.

It was great having him back, though it was nearly dark before he and half the crew arrived. They worked until midnight as if inspired, and I could imagine that we were back on course. The Carpenter did not mention his apostasy, but chatted on about being halfway through *A Farewell to Arms,* and that it was the last war book he was going to read for a while. Too sad and depressing, too full of victims.

When he left, I told him how important it was for me that he complete the job in a few days of consistent work. It had become a matter of grave importance, because every day that we were not open for business we were spending money and not making it. My brother was wondering what was causing the delay. The Carpenter said he understood. He would be back the first thing in the morning. He told the crew the same thing before they left.

I was there at 8:00, before the earliest of our starting times. No one came. Just before 10:00 Mike and his buddy came for the tools. The whole crew had been there at 7:30, he said. I was not there. Justification enough. They had gone to the other job.

While the two workers gathered up the tools, I walked over to what had become the kitchen and began to sift through the stack of time cards piled on the table beside the walk-in freezer. The earliest work had ever begun all summer was 8:20. It was usually around 8:40 or so when they punched in. We were on a cost-plus arrangement, so I kept a close watch on the payroll. 7:30? Yes, I was not there.

As I said before, I told Mike to tell the Carpenter how disappointed I was that things did not work out. As he and the young guy loaded the tools onto their truck and drove away, I looked around at the nearly finished restaurant. The bank had faded into memory, along with the pleasant hours of the Carpenter's presence. A week, maybe two, and customers would fill the spaces with their own stories of promise and disappointment. It would all fit together in the patternless confusion that trickles through our minds and into the stories of our days.

I called the floor people to see if they were still coming in to lay tile. They would be there tomorrow without fail. I went through the list of the carpenters I had rejected. I needed to sift through each of them again, to recruit one to finish the job. I wrote a check for some bills the Carpenter had paid and conjured up a nice letter wishing him well, hoping that he and his wife would find the Path. I suggested *tai chi* as a really good way to enter into relaxing meditation.

As I reached for the phone to begin the process of finding a replacement for the Carpenter, I felt depressed — the way you feel when a trusted colleague has not carried his part of the departmental load, or a long-time neighbor has moved to Omaha. A sense of loss for yourself and for the other. To begin all over again is not easy. I dialed a number, the first on an old list. A man answered. His speech was slurred, and someone was screaming at him in the background. I knew that I was talking to a very reliable carpenter, and that I could count on him but could not count on the others.   ✹

ꓮ Fairy Tale

When Don and I left the meeting we stepped into the end of a cold afternoon of late fall. It was a splendid, clear day, just the opposite of the stuffy workshop room that had surrounded us since early morning. If we moved quickly, we might retrieve his car at the office and still beat the worst of the afternoon traffic — and arrive at our homes at a reasonable hour.

It was not to be. As soon as we whipped onto the perimeter we came to a stop. Traffic was jammed up ahead of us as far as we could see. I looked at Don, grabbed the car phone, and called the office. Bad news. There was a pile-up somewhere, and the perimeter was frozen at a standstill. No thaw in sight.

"And on such a beautiful day," Don mused. "You know, all the leaves have fallen from the trees around our neighborhood. It's kinda bare, but nice. Every day I see something that has been hidden from view since last spring. Sometimes I don't remember it being there. It pops up as a surprise. Maybe it's brand new. There's this gazebo down the street, for instance, that I swear was not there last year. And then other sights return as anticipated — like the brow of the hills and some of the homes that sit way back from the street. Without the trees and shrubs you can even see the people wandering around. It's kinda nice."

I knew what he meant. I thought his description contained a pleasing paradigm for what I would like to experience at a meeting. Or in life. The leaves were like problems that obscure reality. Once you can shake them down, then you can see more clearly the things already there. Next, you discover that exciting, fresh opportunities appear as if from nowhere — and you begin to see that which you have never seen before. Even clients become people. You launch out into the new! The fun begins! Say, I might use that at the next workshop.

We were not moving. I suggested that we make recreational use of the time while it and we were stalled. We were both tired of anxious, goal-centered dialogue. Enough of that all morning. Although we were a good team pair, we were tired of one another and our routines of "same old thing." I searched the CD rack, saw nothing I liked, and suggested that Don choose something. He had an idea. Pulling a CD out of his briefcase, he said, "I bought this from that resources booth before we left. Thought it might be interesting. The description says it's 'an imaginative examination of political systems in large and small organizations.' We could sure use some imagination at our place!"

We still hadn't budged an inch. People in the cars around us were talking on their phones, listening to the radio, or just sinking into the holes in their lives. Whatever hid in the innards of the CD, we could do better than our fellow victims. We'd probably hear the whole thing before we could escape the mess ahead. "Let's hear it," I said. What did we have to lose? I thought. "What's the title?" I asked. "A Fairy Tale," Don said. We both laughed. It started to play:

A CPA with an MBA once gathered his three little children around him and told them this tale:

"Once upon a time, there was a handsome king who was given two beautiful kingdoms — one young, one old. He was happy to be king, for he loved the kingdoms, each in a special way. He had walked among the people as their prince, talking with them and sharing their troubles and their hopes. He had been a very popular prince, so all the people came joyously to his coronation, telling one another that the future had never looked brighter.

"The fields and gardens of the kingdoms produced plenty. The work was hard, and no one was rich, but the people liked hard work and didn't much mind the long hours. The old men said, 'Work is fun when the community of workers and officials of the kingdom love and respect one another and can agree and disagree openly, without fear of recriminations.'

"One day the good king, realizing there was too much work for him to do alone, decided to call a friend from a neighboring kingdom to help. Being of royal blood, the friend was of course made a prince and given power second only to the king's.

"But the new prince was appalled at the primitive, naive practices of his new charges. Farming methods were outdated, based on teamwork and sharing the load. Roads were rough and vehicles were old. Buildings were crowded and without room for expansion. Worst of all, the dukes and duchesses lived as simply as the artisans and peasants. Indeed, some of the peasants had even more than those of royal blood! He was horrified to learn that there was also affectionate fraternizing across class lines. Many lesser officials and servants did not know their places.

"In the meantime, the hills and valleys of the kingdoms continued to produce the finest horses and cows and the most beautiful grains, fruits, and vegetables that could be found anywhere. All the people enjoyed the quality of their products and the quality of their common life together. They viewed it as Excellence.

"But the new prince knew it was time for a change. The hills and valleys could produce more. The people — and officials — could grow much richer. The roads could become highways. Clearly, the entire structure of the kingdoms needed an overhaul.

"When the new prince advised the king of this terrible situation, the king was alarmed. He realized he was no longer in contact with his people, now that he had a prince to take care of that kind of thing. He told the prince to come up with a Master Plan. Perhaps it was not too late to save the kingdoms!

"And so the prince set to work. Remembering how it was where he came from, he sent out orders that all decisions in the kingdoms would henceforth be made by the king — and that he, the prince, was the king's designated spokesman. Soon the prince's desk was piled high with matters awaiting a decision. He realized how slowly the kingdoms were progressing. He saw that he needed to take bold new steps to accelerate progress.

"Within a short time, the prince, acting in the name of the king, fired all the fuddy-duddy, old, quaint, popular officials, re-placing them with people from his former kingdom or others who agreed with him. The main thing they needed to agree upon was that they would never disagree with either the prince or the king. In fact, the new prince soon convinced the king that the need for absolute loyalty would require the establishment of an entirely new Royal Organizational Chart and the hiring of hundreds of new Royal Managers.

"The prince's plan succeeded so well that, before long, the prince couldn't keep up with his newly hired Royal Managers, let alone the hills and the valleys and the horses and the cows and the grain and the vegetables and the fruit. Dozens of bright new programs were started, but nothing was carried through. All the Royal Managers blamed one another when things went wrong. Production dropped, although the hills and valleys were still clamoring to grow beautiful things for the kingdoms.

"It was clear to the prince that a masterly act was called for. The peasants were restless and sullen. Speeches were made in the town squares. Everything the prince did for the common folk seemed to go unappreciated. All this was reported to the king by the prince. The king was getting angrier and angrier at the obviously arrogant rejection by his subjects of his royal good intentions. Yes, a masterly act was in order.

"The Second Royal Reorganization Act was presented by the prince to the king's court, where it passed with applause. The prince pointed out that the problem lay entirely with the old organizational plan. The kingdoms needed to be subdivided into as many parts as possible, with a prince appointed over each of the two kingdoms and an archprince (himself, of course) over the princes. Then, each prince was to hire as many dukes and duchesses as possible — and thus the kingdom would be saved!

"Such bustling and excitement followed! The new archprince and the king appointed the king's jester (and only remaining friend) to become prince of the Old Kingdom. In the face of many protest demonstrations, they appointed an old duke no one knew what else to do with to become prince of the New Kingdom. With the future thus secured, the archprince and the king moved into a newly restored castle on the highest mountain overlooking the valley, traded carriages every year, contrived wonderful festivals and feasts to impress the servants and peasants, and made decisions right and left based on the reports they received from the two princes.

"Then, one day, a terrible thing happened! Hundreds of servants and peasants swarmed out of their cottages and marched upon the castle. A spokesperson presented a petition addressed to the king. It asked for adequate food for the hungry people of both kingdoms. So much food was going to the royal managers and other officials that little was left for the servants and peasants. The petition asked for an honest voice in all matters directly affecting the commoners.

"The king and archprince were furious! They ordered the King's Guard to disperse the mob. The peasants scurried back to their cottages in great fear. Some of them even took their few belongings and fled, by night, to adjoining kingdoms. Those who remained vowed to do only the minimum of work required by the royal managers. They ceased to gather in the town square for parties and dancing and attended royal happenings only when forced to do so, and then reluctantly and without comment.

"With fewer servants and peasants to do the work, it was but a short time before the hills and valleys yielded much less than before. Even the royal managers began to notice that the horses and cattle were not so fat and that the grains, fruit, and vegetables were of poorer quality. Campaigns were launched to rave and rant about the pursuit of excellence, but nothing changed.

"And then one day the Royal Managers discovered that only the servants and peasants who were sick or trying to gain royal status were left in the kingdoms to do the work. In each kingdom, the Royal Managers complained to their prince about conditions. The princes were certainly not going to accept responsibility for the situation, so they blamed it on the king and the archprince. This did not satisfy the servants and the peasants, and it made the king and the archprince red with anger. In fact, they blamed the princes, the servants, and the peasants for everything!

"And then the prince of the Old Kingdom saw a way out. He decided to blame the prince and servants and people of the New Kingdom for the terrible conditions. Before the New Kingdom knew what was happening, the army of the Old Kingdom joined with the King's Guard in a sudden and effective attack upon the unsuspecting New Kingdom. In a week it was all over, and the Royal Managers in the New Kingdom had been thrown in irons and replaced by officials from other kingdoms far away. All the servants and peasants were arrested and put into labor camps for the duration of the emergency.

"Of course, as you might suspect by now, the cost of the great bureaucracy and the military campaign soon combined to throw both kingdoms into a desperate financial plight. For a time the archprince kept things going by selling off the hills and valleys to developers from foreign kingdoms, but soon only a small, garden-size patch of land was left in each kingdom.

"When the king realized that his kingdoms had shrunk to such a tiny size, he felt very sad. He remembered the Good Old

Days when he used to walk among the people and enjoy their friendship and praise. He couldn't understand why they had become so ungrateful that they would contribute to such a disaster. Now he was shocked to realize that the only subjects left in either kingdom were his Royal Managers and a few grumbling slaves who had once been servants and peasants.

"The king called in his archprince for a conference. He told the archprince that he wanted to bring back the Good Old Days. The archprince said that was impossible. In fact, he told the king he must move out of the palace the following week, because it had been sold to a kingdom developer to pay the salaries of the soldiers and Royal Managers who were left in the two tiny kingdoms. The archprince went on to say that it was all the king's fault, that he, the archprince, had carried out the king's orders long enough, and that the King's Guards were now loyal to the archprince and had taken control of a new government, in which the king would be merely a symbolic leader.

"At last the king took in the full import of what had happened. He sprang to his feet, pulled his trusty sword from its scabbard, and plunged it into the body of the leering archprince! Then, the strangest thing happened! Can you guess the ending?"

The three little children, their mouths open and their eyes wide, caught a quick breath at the excitement and mystery of the situation in the story. They thought for a moment, and then the youngest said,

"I know! The archprince turned into a frog and hopped out the castle window, never to be seen again!"

The middle child said,

"No, silly, that's not what happened. The king went out and killed all the guards, rounded up the people who were left, and got them all together, and then they killed all the mean old Royal Managers and set the slaves free and started all over again and lived happily ever after in the Good Old Days!"

The oldest child, who had remained silent, finally said, "No, you're neither one right. I'll bet the story has no ending at all. It starts over again from the beginning, like a CD in the car CD player. Tell us, Father, am I right?"

The father looked at his eldest in amazement, then took them all in his arms and hugged them tight. With a flutter in his throat, he said, "In a way, I suppose all three of you are right. I've never known for sure just how the story came out myself. Perhaps it hasn't ended, yet. Maybe that's just the way with fairy tales these days."

By the time the story was over we were off the perimeter and through the shortcuts to the office, and Don was climbing out of my car, ready to climb into his own.

"Well, ol' Prince," he chided, "see you tomorrow at what's left of the palace."

"It takes a Prince to know a Prince," I grinned back. "But it's up to you to straighten out the Archprince and the King." I realized, as he got into his car, that I was serious about that.   ✹

Bag-Boy Willie

Thus far, I am alone in the little park. The others have not arrived. Yet. The park is only itself and me. This park is an offering that struggled, misshapen and yet somehow formed, from the discord of the town council. A compromise between retrenchment and expansion, of fear and hopeful dreams. It is home to a walking track, a pavilion, and a children's playground. All exactly half the size of the lone liberal's proposal and half again the size of the pinched plan of the conservatives.

In the far corner, a weeping willow genuflects, inspired by the nudging breeze of a summer morning. Its fingertips stroke the waking surface of the stream that nurtures its roots. I pretend the gracefully waving branches of the delicate tree are my fingers, their unstained touch the sensation I might have if I were to stroke hope or love or the soft-skinned tops of clouds. And I wonder what Willie sees and feels at this moment. What do his fingers touch?

I leave the walking track that binds the little park, carefully drift down a gentle slope, then crouch on the bank of the narrow stream that holds one side of the park in place. Sometimes two muskrats play in the shade of the tree — before the stillness that holds the breath of day bows to the troubled speech of business-as-usual and retires to sanctuaries of moving shadows to await the night.

This morning the mischievous, beaverlike muskrats are there. Cupped in the willow's shadows, they chase the sun-twinkles that sift through the supple generosity of the willow's branches. Twisting and turning like my sleek and careless thoughts when I laugh, they bump and scamper, touch and retreat, connect and reclaim their freedom. Blending at times with the playful, darker, cool splotches beneath the water's slowly moving surface, they find fleeting hideaways to cover their antics. Then they zestfully reappear as dancing, frothy splashes.

I cannot return to my morning walk. I must watch, huddling inside my moment while venturing into theirs. I had come to the park to walk, compelled by the belief that I would realize more of myself if I would begin the day with a hustling walk. Good preparation for a hustling day. All days hustle. I am at that age. I am a hustler.

I had come to the park to celebrate my breathing and mobility, to affirm my gifts of flowing blood and obedient heart. I could feel the soles of my feet sending messages to my brain that I was in touch. In touch with the solid earth, the spinning globe, the floating universe, the unreachable beyond. In touch with the little park in the obscure village where I was becoming the next thing that I might be.

I had left the touch of my bed, my wife sleeping. I was only here. This could be the end, the final touching, the place between the touches that were yesterday and the touches that would never happen. I wondered what Willie touched at this hour. I watched the muskrats. Their touch was wet, fluid, short-lived. But what was mine? I could only be sure that we were becoming something together, each without a certain plan for touching.

Then other walkers reached the park. They began to dot the track and set time in motion again, pushing and shoving my thoughts with their aggressive striding. Things were getting complicated. Walkers come in two species: clockwise and counterclockwise. I am a counterclockwise person. I believe that I am right. It is only when I am thinking that I venture into the realm of clockwiseness. It is dangerous, for it propels me into another view of reality. I might encounter Others from the front rather than from behind. I might change the way I see them and things.

The walkers stopped to see what I was watching. Being civilized, they gathered and began to speak. "See the muskrats!" The conversation commenced, and the picture started to fade. Descriptions and opinions followed each "Oh, look!" — but none saw the same thing, and they began to think less of one another as their visions hung separately, dividing them into ones. I wondered what Willie would say.

I was pulled back into the emerging morning of another day. The sun sucked the remaining mists from the park grass. What had been lurking reality all along now reappeared in its harshest vestments. The muskrats knew. They fled. I wanted to follow them, but I did not know where to go. How did they so easily know of another place?

Then I saw him. The moment I put my foot back on the track I saw him, appearing out of a world strange to me and to which I am uninvited, processing like alien royalty into the swirling kingdom of the rising morning sounds. Small head. Round belly. Short, fat legs springing from tiny feet. Wisp of black mustache clinging to the short space between lip and nose. It was Willie, the bagboy at Howard's Supermarket.

Just beyond the stream, through the willow, up the bank and over the railroad bed I saw him. He walked his strange walk, short arms dangling as if hastily stuck to his shoulders as a congenital afterthought, flopping confidently out of rhythm with the picky staccato of his steps.

His head held high, he was a giant child on his way to being a team member at Howard's Supermarket. He had been chosen before all worlds to be a member of the gang. He was nothing at all until chosen to play on the team. Howard's was the exact point of the center of the universe, and he had been chosen to work there. His position was bag-boy. He was the only Bag-Boy Willie ever created.

The street had become busy. The semi's and pickup trucks and mostly old-model cars hastily recreated the icon of our rural village for another day. Willie's gait hummed the same raspy music sung by the churning trailer wheels. He was at one with the irritated pickups as they beeped chaotic messages of desire to get on with it. He was on his way, too. He, too, was going to work. His eyes were wide and proud. At work, people counted on him. Every day, seven days a week, holidays too. "What would we do without you, Willie?" He told them — with a look of anxious concern for their existence — that he didn't know.

Willie was the only employee remaining of the crew he had started with, eight years before. In and out of all those years, he had ignored the political and interpersonal struggles of the super-market. Arguments between managers, employees, and customers flowed around him as softly and harmlessly as the water in the park stream caressed the muskrats. He swam in it, played in it as if provided by God. As if he had special underwater breathing capacities that all others lacked.

Each customer was his for a fleeting lifetime. Covered by the gracious branches of his job description, he dove and turned and twisted and splashed through joyous days in the shade or in the sun. It mattered not at all the weather or the time of day. No matter which man was boss. No matter the teasing of the schoolboys who thought they were skilled enough to be bag-boys for a while — until they tired of it and quit. They always quit. They always had some meaningless complaint, as if they were comparing the life of a bag-boy with something else. But what could that be? "What a waste of time," they muttered. Willie was the bag-boy of all bag-boys. No matter what. Eternally.

No one could place groceries properly in a bag like Willie. The eggs never broke. The frozen-food packages never sweated onto other foods. The fragile lettuce leaves always peeped safely from the top of the bag. Cans jostled cans, but not too many in any one bag. Nothing heavy or sharp ever mashed or scraped the thin-skinned tomatoes. Bread was always safe from attack. No bag was too heavy. No bag was wasted. Willie was, indeed, the Bag-Boy Supreme.

In our village, the bag-boys wheel the grocery carts, packed with their stuffed plastic or brown-paper sacks, through the automatic doors and out to the waiting trucks and cars. There they are placed on seats or in trunks — with varying skill. Newcomers to the village who are used to fending for themselves have to get used to this unexpected service. Signs say "Do Not Tip," but, as in the case of most of the laws in our county, we are free to disregard the instructions and do as we like.

When the groceries are finally stashed away, and the customer is about to leave, there is always a slight pause which includes the phrase, "Thank you for shopping at Howard's Supermarket." No hand is put out in expectation of a tip. If a tip is offered, it is gratefully received and slipped into an apron pocket. But when Willie receives a tip, a spontaneous liturgy begins. His face lights up like a round bulb of delighted surprise. His little mustache almost disappears up his thick, flat nose. His "Thank you!" turns the giver into a world-class philanthropist. His deep-set eyes shine like beacons as he clasps coin or bill between his two hands and deeply bows, like a doting prince before his king or queen. And if no tip is offered, he smiles broadly, invites his customers back, and waves his pudgy right hand in priestly blessing as they leave.

Many customers admit they come to Howard's because of Willie. They will try to beat the crowd, or jockey for position in the line, in an effort to get him to bag their groceries and push their carts. He spots regular customers, tagging them with a sidelong look and serious expression. He is drawn to frail old ladies and anyone else in obvious need of assistance. Howard's has the slowest lines and the most confused, erratic service in the community. But all agree that it has the best bag-boy anyone has ever seen.

I stand beside the track now and watch Willie. He is already in uniform, neatly dressed in clean white shirt and khaki trousers. A brown apron strains to cover his bulging front. He wears the apron everywhere he goes. It reads "Shop at Howard's and Save" in faded white script located in the neighborhood of his belly button. Willie washes his precious apron every night and irons it himself every morning.

His minimum wage has not changed in eight years — except on the one occasion when the law required it, and he was "advanced" to a new minimum wage. But he gets a new apron every two months. When it arrives and he turns in his old one, there is a solemn ceremony of exchange. Willie calls this his "promotion." He has been "promoted" more than anyone in the history of the Howard's Supermarket chain. Maybe more than anyone anywhere.

Willie waits at the railroad crossing beside the County First Bank for the traffic light to halt the growing vehicular parade. Then he walks with gallant determination across the street and into the supermarket's parking lot. The sun is already hot as the expectant automatic doors swing wide for him, and he strides majestically into the cool, welcoming interior. He will soon grasp his own time-card, confidently approach the gray, calculating clock-machine that purports to measure his worth, and punch in. Within an instant he will become the complete Bag-Boy Willie. He will begin another day of being — another day of being here. Touching the earth. Touching the globe. Touching the universe. Touching all of existence with pure moments of bag-boyness.

I look down again at the surface of the stream. It is almost still, empty. The muskrats took their memory with them. The sun begins to heat the surface and coat it with a heavy cosmic glaze. The willow branches have shifted their shade to places less likely to produce magic. The heat turns up a notch toward summer. I know I must resume my laps around the track. I'll make at least one, maybe more.

But I'll deal with such decisions when I get there. For now, I have the track and the park. A place to be. The muskrats have gone on to their next place, forgetting where they've been. And Willie, too, is embracing his primordial identity, being the best of all bag-boys for one more day. We are all being drawn toward the unknown that awaits us beyond our moments of meaning.

As I step onto the track again, I scan the street, the traffic, and hear the noises of life that seem so important. I know this is the place where I will try to survive. But the muskrats will not survive if I don't decide to protect them from myself and the other walkers.

And Willie. Will he survive? He has been "part-time" with overtime for eight years, so he has never been eligible for raises or health care and has no retirement benefits. These facts sift through the inbred genes of his mild retardation and physical distortions. They do not catch on any understanding that requires measurement against ethical standards or a place beneath the canopies of morality. I think about the fuzzy carelessness of this method of honoring brothers and sisters and friends.

I think of innocence. I think of myself. I think that there must have been an innocent time for me. There must have been, or how could I imagine its having been? I recognize the innocence of the muskrats playing in the shadow of the willow and seem to remember the experience from somewhere else. Did I recollect that moment of frivolous, natural beauty from some other time? Was I either swimming as one of the muskrats, or did I give shade as a willow tree, or move toward an end as a stream? I can't recall.

And Willie. I wonder why I suddenly wish that I could walk this track in the park with the divine, myopic assurance of his innocence. Could I be feeling connections with life lived without the sophisticated apparatus of judging, valuing, believing, pursuing the tail of my culture? Is there within me the genetic map that could guide me to become the best bag-boy in town? In the county? On the globe? In the universe? But who would be there to protect me from the managers, the teasers, and the users of others' lives? Could I survive?

I follow the outline of the track for another round. I touch the earth, spin with the globe, float with the universe. I see the park, walk within its boundaries, and know it as my place for the moment. Eventually I will have enough of the reality I have come to sense. When that happens, I will try something else, I announce to a tiny spot deep within me.

Perhaps, I say to myself, I will become submerged in something beautiful. Something innocent. Like swimming with muskrats. Or working with Willie. Yes. He would let me wear his brown apron that declares "Shop at Howard's and Save." And he might teach me the fundamental bag-boy ceremonies of life — and the liturgy of receiving a tip of universal size.   ✸

The Last Great USO Dance

It has been a long time since those USO dances in Manila. The war was barely over then. The waiting had just begun. Waiting to come home, for points to pile up, for saying goodbye to the heat and the rain and the stopping of time. When I could, I hitchhiked into Manila for the USO dances. The Filipino girls were good dancers.

I liked Aida Limjoco and her sister best. They would invite me home, chaperoned by their older brother. Their Chinese-ancestored father liked me, and we had long talks. We ate dinner at a real table with real tableware. Mr. Limjoco had attended Columbia University in New York City before the war. He had stories to tell, about NYC — and about hiding his family under a peasant's disguise in a little northern village during the war.

We talked a lot about education. He planned to send his children to the United States for college. In fact, Aida graduated from a California university years later. Mr. Limjoco wanted to know where I intended to go to college when I got home. I didn't know. I didn't even know when I was going home. First things first. And I didn't know about college. I didn't have any money and college was expensive. I simply didn't know.

That was fifty years ago. And now there was to be a special alumni day at my college for those of us who were in World War II. It was advertised as "The Last Great USO Dance." A long time between USO dances. Many other dances in between. G.I. Bill and college. Marriage and family. Preaching, teaching and writing. Swing and sway. Grandchildren encores. And then — The Last Great USO Dance, college alumni day, 1995.

We gathered at the new outdoor social area: pavilion and dance floor, tables and USO banners, authentic 1945. I danced like a crazy man, age 19 and 69. The "replica" Andrews Sisters were perfect. "Boogie-Woogie Bugle Call!" Yeah! Now was becoming then. It was all the same. I'm a better dancer now, but, like then, wet with sweat halfway through the Jersey Bounce.

It began to rain. Unscheduled, like all the rest of things for fifty years. We opened the umbrella I said it was silly to bring. We kept on dancing. It was The Last Great USO Dance. No tune could be missed. Even in the rain. "Serenade in Blue." Slow, close dancing. Don't go away. One more. "Tuxedo Junction." Go wild. Remember. Hiroshima. Nagasaki. Louder. More!

I heard there was a movie showing at an artillery headquarters unit nearby. We talked the Old Man out of a two-and-a-half-ton truck and slithered through the Philippine mud. The rains came. Again. Still. Forever, the rains. Liking the night. Not afraid of the night like we were. Japs were still tucked away in the hills, shivering in their lost dreams. Like us, afraid. But with no movies.

Like turtles, we ducked our helmeted heads into our poncho necks, leaving a slit to see through. We sat sloppy wet in the mud on the side of a hill. With all the other sloppy wet turtles. Our carbines hid safely under our ponchos. Lauren Bacall and Humphrey Bogart were dry. Their voices warm. They spoke to us from beneath the overhang of the makeshift stage someone had thrown together to shelter the screen. To shelter the pilot light of romance that needed protection deep in our souls. To shelter the tiny flame of dreams we hoped would come true. "To Have and To Have Not" was the film. 1945 the year. August tenth the day.

And the rains came. Ping and swoosh, the sound track on my head. Not much hair left. Keep the umbrella over us. Don't worry about me. I'm already wet. Great band. "In the Mood." Jesus! We'll stay for the last dance. John's just sitting over there, tapping his foot. Can't dance. Knee surgery. Billy stands there, watching. Did he ever dance? I can't remember. Where are the others, the Class of 1950? Coleman could dance if he would. Nothing to be afraid of, guys. No ponchos now, except the covering of the years and memories of our becoming. Hardly rain-proof. Keep dancing. The band plays on.

The Lieutenant stopped the movie. Right when it was getting interesting, and I was forgetting I was wet. It rained harder. We booooooed! We cursed. Bastard! Why did he stop the Bogart right in the middle of the story, in the middle of the night, in the middle of the Philippines, in the middle of my anger at soldiering, in the middle of my trying to stay dry? We were too young for the movie to stop. Not now!

The Lieutenant shouted at the rain: "The Japs have accepted Potsdam! The war is over! We're going home!" Holy Cow! They stopped the dance. The band started to put away the saxophones and trumpets, threw the trombones into their cases, piled everything into a huge mess, tossed it all on a truck and got the hell out of there. The dance was over.

The boy-becoming-man fired his carbine into the dark, liberated, torrential sky. Shouted, screamed at the mud and hate. He began to drown in the deluge of an ended war. Strangling with the thousand thoughts of going home. In the rain. Who cares? We are not dead. Taste the rain. We are still alive. And the war is over. Can we dance in the rain? Under an umbrella? Two won't fit under one poncho, but we can try. Let us dance, and fire carbines at the night.

A day of victory! We made it! The Last Great USO Dance.

1995. Still crazily alive. Still dancing. It's still raining all around, but don't worry. They will stop the dance just in time. My hearing aids have shorted out from rain and sweat. I must not forget to take my cholesterol pill and toss down the voodoo capsules for my prostate. I'll hit the john before we start home. Will you be here when I get back?

I was stuck in the Philippines, stuck in time, collecting "points" that would earn me a ticket home. I waited so long there came an end to waiting. But you can dance while waiting. You can go to the USO in Manila every chance you get. You can dance with Aida, and talk with Mr. Limjoco. You can wonder when the USO dances will stop. You can wonder how to answer Mr. Limjoco's questions about school and life.

I was finally discharged from the chaos I had learned to manage and was pointed toward the unknown next steps. G.I. Bill? What's that? Go where? Sounds good to me.

I caught the trolley to downtown. The Captain who shook my hand goodbye had said that if I transferred to the trolley that said "University" and went to the end of the line, I could start college. Why not?

The mud was waiting. They were fixing the walkway. Walk in the mud, soldier. Patted with spring rain, I hunched through the University gates with my life's possessions in a duffle-bag on my shoulder. I told the man that I wanted to go to college like Mr. Limjoco said. "Who?" he asked. "Never mind," I said. "I just want to go to college." And I did.

And it kept on raining. Not the old kind of rain, the kind you think you will drown in, wondering if all of life is to be forever wet and full of night. A new kind of rain. The kind that is soft and warm, that nourishes and causes new life to grow. The college had the right kind of soil for me, and just enough of the right kind of rain. Opportunities. Mentors. Hope. Sunny days, too.

I've often wondered how the movie came out. I guess I could find it and see. It's a classic, I'm told. But maybe it's best left unfinished. Like The Last Great USO Dance. Like the sound of the Big Band. Like the memories of war. Like friendships fifty years old. Like our dancing together to "Moonlight Mood." Like Alumni Day 1995. Like this little life of mine. And yours. And the rain.

The Enchanted Vision

It was my first morning walk in my new mountain neighborhood. Summer — still yet unknown neighbors asleep or early stirring; still cool enough for the air to rest gently on the million surfaces of green leaves.

I turned down a gradual, sloping street dotted with several homes. Flowered yards and gracious porches stamped them with the luxuries of beauty and hospitality. I swung my walking stick, pretending to match the rhythmic sounds of growing plants and nature's patience.

In one yard I noticed a life-size facsimile of a stunning six-point buck. Alert, head erect and slightly turned, he had been placed by his owners in the middle of their yard, comfortably blending with shrubs, trees, and early shadows.

And then he seemed to turn his head a quarter move, and his eyes met mine. His black nose twitched and his ample lips smiled. I stopped, no more than a hundred feet away, and smiled back, amused at myself at being caught by an illusion of life. I wondered how often the realities of my life were animated perceptions of rigid human icons — whether it could be that all I had learned to believe was like a ceramic sculpture standing in the garden of my culture, speckled with the camouflage of life's few mornings.

Still caught on the neutral, indulgent stare of the tall, brown-gray figure, I stepped forward again, striding toward the cul-de-sac at the street's end. It was then that he moved. All of him.

Without haste, unconcerned as a soft summer's shadow, he turned his head from me and toward his future; he glided without fear or comment on my presence, entering the waiting woods and floating out of my sight, into discovery.

"Ahhhh!" I said aloud, rejoicing at what had been such a magical morning moment! The bare reason of my mind gave way to the joyous emotion of discovery once again: that what is seen as lifeless can have new life; that perception must appreciate the artifices of culture, searching for the illusion while enlivening it with fresh meaning; that all that is holy is caught in the process of becoming.

I walked on. No, I strutted, I pranced. When I was sure no one was watching, I even danced! And I said to myself: Listen to the voice of the morning. I listened, and I heard triumphant words that flew through the valleys like the shout of Dawn: "Behold, I make all things new!"

Reaching the lip of a ridge, I paused. The lofty blue-green mountain crests hovered patiently all around me, enclosing my instant in their primordial memory. I saw myself from a distance, poised in the midst of an immense, rambling garden, a sculpture given life without illusion, an incarnate vision ready to disappear into the enchanted woodlands of my days.

Jerry Zeller is available for:

 prose or poetry readings

 workshops on interpersonal communications

 spiritual retreats, in joint leadership with his wife Pat

call
(706) 692-5842

Recovery Communications, Inc.

BOOK PUBLISHING & AUTHOR PROMOTIONS

Post Office Box 19910
Baltimore, Maryland 21211, USA

Now available through your local bookstore!

Jennifer J. Richardson, M.S.W. *Diary of Abuse/Diary of Healing.* A young girl's secret journal recording two decades of abuse, with detailed healing therapy sessions. A very raw and extraordinary book. **Contact the author at: (404) 373-1837.**

Toby Rice Drews. *Getting Them Sober, Volume One — You Can Help!* Hundreds of ideas for sobriety and recovery. The million-seller endorsed by Melody Beattie, Dr. Norman Vincent Peale, and "Dear Abby." **Contact the author at: (410) 243-8352.**

Toby Rice Drews. *Getting Them Sober, Volume Four — Separation Decisions.* All about detachment and separation issues for families of alcoholics. Endorsed by Max Weisman, M.D., past president of the American Society of Addiction Medicine. **Contact the author at: (410) 243-8352.**

Betsy Tice White. *Turning Your Teen Around — How A Couple Helped Their Troubled Son While Keeping Their Marriage Alive and Well.* A doctor family's successful personal battle against teen-age drug use, with dozens of powerfully helpful tips for parents in pain. Endorsed by John Palmer, NBC News. **Contact the author at: (770) 590-7311.**

Betsy Tice White. *Mountain Folk, Mountain Food — Down-Home Wisdom, Plain Tales, and Recipe Secrets from Appalachia.* The joy of living as expressed in charming vignettes and mouth-watering regional foods! Endorsed by the host of the TV series "Great Country Inns" and by *Blue Ridge Country Magazine.* **Contact the author at: (770) 590-7311.**

Joseph L. Buccilli, Ph.D. *Wise Stuff About Relationships.* A gem of a book for anyone in recovery; "an empowering spiritual workout." Endorsed by the vice president of the *Philadelphia Inquirer.* **Contact the author at: (609) 629-4441.**

Linda Meyer, Ph.D. *I See Myself Changing — Weekly Meditations and Recovery Journaling for Young Adults.* A life-affirming book for adolescents and young adults, endorsed by Robert Bulkeley, The Gilman School. **Contact the author at: (217) 367-8821.**

John Pearson. *Eastern Shore Beckonings.* Marvelous trek back in time through charming villages and encounters with solid Chesapeake Bay folk. "Aches with affection" — the *Village Voice's* Washington correspondent. **Contact the author at: (410) 315-7940.**

AND COMING SOON . . . .

David E. Bergesen. *Murder Crosses the Equator — A Father Jack Carthier Mystery.* Volcanic tale of suspense in a Latin-American setting, starring a clever missionary-priest detective.

Stacie Hagan and Charlie Palmgren. *The Chicken Conspiracy — Breaking the Cycle of Personal Stress and Organizational Mediocrity.* A liberating message from corporate trainers about successful personal, organizational, and global change.

Mattie Carroll Mullins. *Judy — The Murder of My Daughter, The Healing of My Family.* A Christian mother's inspiring story of how her family moved from unimaginable tragedy to forgiveness.